For my friends and family, particularly Stephi, with special thanks to Steve, Christian and Petra for their help.

AF281675

Rossiter, Andrew:
Apricot Juice and Other Stories /Andrew Rossiter
Hamburg, Germany; 2000
ISBN: 3-8311-1274-6

Cover Design: Steve Wilson & Andrew Rossiter
Photography: Steve Wilson
Copyright © Andrew Rossiter 2000

Printed in Germany

Apricot Juice and Other Stories

Andrew Rossiter was born in Newport Gwent in 1964. While completing a PhD in Philosophy at Middlesex University he moved to Hamburg where he worked in a drug advisory centre. This debut book is based around his experiences there.

APRICOT JUICE AND OTHER STORIES

BY

ANDREW ROSSITER

Contents

APRICOT JUICE

Apricot Juice and Other Stories...

Hamburg. So-called second home of the Beatles. Ever seen the Hamburg Beatles' museum? Piled up pieces of nostalgic shit, plus one old grainy film. And all for the handsome price of five shiny marks. Best keep your marks and buy a beer. The bars of Hamburg portray their own dubious attractions - and who really gives a toss about the Beatles today, 'cept for those pretty bad boys from Oasis. But if you're not going anywhere special, neither up nor down, but just sidling along, then I would recommend the bars of Hamburg as as good as place as any to do it in. Enough money going round to give the illusion of luxury, but not enough to create that paranoid lock out and chain up mentality of having too much.

'Course, we're all nobodies. Neither the hard and flash of the old working class, nor the smug and successful of the well to do middle class, but 'least we can dream of being one or the other. A Traumwelt where we can still fancy ourselves our own little kind of heroes and heroines without fear of the dull thud of some blunt instrument or the iron flash of bloodied concrete. No wonder there are so many fucked up people here.

It was, on reflection, a mistake to go into the "Cocteau." I was due to meet some people for a little indulgence of the liquid sort. Trouble was, they weren't too sure of their choice of bar. So I guess it was just a case of me checking out the usual places 'till I found them. Only problem with this routine is meeting people you know but don't really want to see. And that's what happened in the "Cocteau."

I wandered in, trying to look casual and at ease, as you tend to do when going into a bar to look for people. But all you feel like is a little lost kid wondering where all the familiar faces have disappeared to. I stood just inside the doorway and scanned the place as quick as I could, trying to avoid the looks which automatically accompany the opening of a bar door. You nearly always get some wanker checking you out, giving you that halfways condescending, halfways pitying stare that says - sorry mate, no friends here, please piss off. I guess hardly anyone ever thinks that when administering this look. Hell, they probably don't even know they're giving it they done it so often. But that doesn't make you feel any better when you get it.

Seeing Thorsten boring a conversational hole into Kurt's head should've turned me straight round and out the door. But I stand there gawping like a maced macaw at the two bobbing heads, paralysed by the thought of going over. A little too long, as it turns out, because, inevitably, the choice was no longer mine. "Hei Niiick!..."

Thorsten's shout sliced through the room like the cry before a brawl as he glanced towards me. His eyes were tranced out in, what I suppose was for him, a warm smile, but appeared edged with a disturbing glaze of madness. He was one of those blokes whose tone of voice and turn of eye could get him into trouble while he was actually being friendly. And he wasn't the sort to back off either. You know the type. Him and his mates were all like that, a bit damaged in the head. Always chewing things over and around, talking about what they felt or what they thought 'till it got weird or mad. Then they'd lose it and all they'd have was a face shorn of everything 'cept aggro. Then you got out the way. Fast. Thorsten might've been the worst of them, him and his crowd, then again maybe not, but he'd got no limits. Serious limitations yeah, but no limits, no stopping him when he was on to one - that's what made him happy. Or miserable, as the case may be. It was this violence in his smile which caught me. So, with a shrug, I sauntered on over to say Hi, but Thorsten was already back to his drilling mission.

I stood there, unable to interrupt, and too unsure just to go, a state of mind which, on that evening, I couldn't take for long. So I took the easiest of routes and tapped Kurt on his thick leathered shoulder. He swung his hung head to me, still nodding from his mate's barrage, and his face erupted into a warm grin. I like this man.

"Hey, how you doing?" he asks. He's a big bloke with heavy hands, who could've probably bust my arm with a twist of one of them. Thinking about it, Thorsten probably could've too. But the way the words roll down off Kurt's tongue, their ends trailing off in the smoke of his ever present Camel, you get the impression he wouldn't hurt a fucking jelly baby, let alone a fly.

"Alright, I guess." I say. Thorsten's looking over now since it's obvious that someone else is on the scene, but I concentrate on Kurt as he asks what I'm doing here and I answer, "I'm looking for Michaela and the others, you seen 'em at all? No? I'm going to try the 'Dschungel' later on, if you want to drop by..."

But Thorsten's on track and butts straight in there, "Hey, are those two babes from yesterday going to be there? They weren't bad..."

I answer him quick just to stop the monologue on my two friends which was threatening to follow, but just maybe a bit too quick, "Yeah, yeah, probably, but who knows..."

He nods his head enthusiastically, "hey, they weren't bad those two, were they eh? Brilliant evening yesterday. Oh Man, I was so smashed, but bloody brilliant. Alright, we've got something to talk over here, but I might be along later. Say hello to them if you them. See you, then."

And that was it, a quick flash of teeth, accom-panied by a hiccup of a laugh, and I was cordially dismissed from the rank and file of Thorsten Wasleck. I turned to Kurt, patting him once more on the shoulder. At the same time I noticed the baby greys curled up amongst his tight knit hair and a phrase from a crap American soap going through my head "Hey Jake, we're not kids anymore." I brushed it aside, and told him he should come to the "Dschungel," (pronounced "Jungle"). It was this piece of advice which later made me regret ever having gone into the "Cocteau."

I eased my way out of the bar, negotiating the small but thick forest of the high bar stools and tall tables which always make me feel a bit of a dwarf when I go into a bar in Hamburg. I hit the Wohlwill Straße heading off in the opposite direction to the Reeperbahn towards Schulterblatt and the Schanzenviertel. It was already dark, about half past ten, but the air was still thick and warm on my face. It hadn't rained in over a week and the summer stench of piss and dog shit kissed the back of my nose and made me wish for the thunderstorm hanging over the city. I crossed the street to avoid walking past the dark entrance of the small park - a totally unnecessary manoeuvre here in Hamburg, but then again, who knows anyway.

The other evening with Thorsten and the girls was turning over in my mind. Like how he'd gabbled on, and how I was going to explain to them that this especially liberated young man might not only turn up at the bar, but might even find them attractive to boot. I wasn't sure whether it was that I really didn't like him, or it was just his peculiar way with words which got on my tits.

Now a few of them had said they might be going to the "Egal" bar. This was a real pit of a place, a low budget job run by a few hash heads, with no pumps, next to no lights, holes in the floor, and the next generation of alks and junks. Its name means 'who gives a shit,' and it looks like it, but I thought I might see either Clemens or they might be there anyway. After meeting Thorsten I didn't give too much of a shit who I met so it seemed like the right place to try. Near the end of the Wohlwill Straße I took a right, going up the Feldstraße, wide like a fat man's backside after the narrow back street with its thin speed tucks and close-to buildings.

This road is famous, or infamous depending on your point of view, for three things: St. Pauli football club, the Dom (pronounced Dome) with its seasonally alternating fairground and various circuses, and last but not least, ye olde bombe shelter. The first two are both periodic, (but shame they have to be perpetually periodic). Their concerns are the beautifully thronging, fucked up masses of the former working classes which once teemed the ex-BRD and the ex-DDR. I say the former, because the first, we are told, never really existed, whereas the latter are now, by and large, no longer working. But it's the bomb shelter, or the Bunker as it's called, which does it for me.

It's a brown squatting toad of a building whose sense of humour cracks me up. I mean, it's not one of your pissy little Morris shelters which we got taught about in school. And I know they talk about the Germans doing things right, but this is really totally over the top. It was built to house the neighbouring area, is seven storeys high, measuring about two hundred yards the one side by one hundred the other (I never measured, but it looks that way), is built out of reinforced concrete, with black grey walls, and a dirty sand coloured parapet roof. But it's so fucking ugly you've got to smile when you see it. It's got to be one of the best monuments to the war I've ever seen. But the joke is that of course now, what with fifty years after and all that shit, they want to get rid of this eyesore. Of course, this thing was built to take on yer all-American five hundred pounder, and isn't about to let a couple of pissy little demolition experts have their way with it. They built this thing so heavy that if you blow it up the resulting subsidence would make every house situated within five hundred yards unlivable. So the lovely toad's got to stay put. Vorsprung durch Technik, that's what I say.

Past the toady old reminder of really more violent times and turn left into the Glaßhüttenstraße. This street was the place of my old abode, number 101, as in room 101 from 1984, but without the rats and maybe some of the pain, but that's a story for another day as they say in the movies. It belongs to the Karo-viertel - the diamond quarter - which used to house the workers from the nearby docks and the massive slaughter house which blocks off one end of the quarter. Nowadays, of course, the lowing screech and squeal of condemned animals is no longer heard. It's been replaced by the tarmac crumbling rumble of articulated lorries as they lumber their ice cold animal carcasses to and from the few remaining cold storage warehouses. And, of course, these'll be closed down in a matter of months. And, of course, the city wants to convert the whole complex to some kind of yuppie haven, with supercool offices and flats and restaurants and saunas. Almost a kilometre of yuppie shit which no yuppie will want to buy or use because it's right next to the Karo-viertel, which is no place for your average yuppie, if you know what I mean.

I walk the street with its high terraced houses which lean back and look down on you from their flat faced five storeys and set back doorways which provide convenient shelter for a quiet smoke in the rain or a piss in the dark. A couple of Romas with their regulation long black hair and baggy pants strut swiftly in my direction, but they've got their own business to see to so I just move to the side and they strut on by. They're all kids, fourteen or fifteen, but wired high with their own violent importance in their hard little world of petty extortion, mugging, stealing and dealing and you stay out of their way as best you can. Strange how they always walk the street, always fast, and never really together, but in a slanted triangle, with one in front turning his head to talk to the others who flank him, but a little behind.

I crossed the small square toward the "Egal Bar" whose entrance lies adjacent to that of the Oriental. This square forms the social centre of the quarter on warm summer days, crowded with the long rickety clap together tables and benches belonging to the "Café Oriental." After ten o' clock all the bars in Hamburg have to pack away their street paraphernalia. This means that on a summer night you often encounter piles of cheap fold down tables and plastic chairs chained uselessly to the nearest tree or signpost, often confusing wayward dogs and gentleman that they are the cities new urinals.

Cloaking the entrance of the bar is a heavy blue

velvet curtain, stiff with age and spittle and god knows what else. I pushed it back to let the fetid air of endless cigarettes, joints, spilt beer and sawdusted vomit warm itself outside. They've obviously got problems paying the electric, the only real light coming from a dim forty watt bulb hanging belligerently over the bar area, the rest being provided by the little mounds of molten wax which pass as candles. Actually most of the bars in Hamburg use this romantic method of giving their guests lung cancer. And, naturally, the candles are not generally there for their lighting qualities, but to provide something to play with whilst engaging in stunningly boring conversation. A straight backed candle is a sight not often seen since most have been deformed by the artistic whims of would be sculpturists. In the 'Egal' bar, this absence of light has the added advantage of letting its more worthwhile visitors remain in a state of grace as to the real state of the establishment they have ventured into, not to mention obscuring its more common frequenters from themselves.

Standing at the bar were three of my colleagues, unfortunately, as I noted with a feeling that this was going to be a long and probably drunken trawl, not the ones I was looking for. They were OK, and normally I would've stopped for a drink with them, but they weren't really my crowd and I wasn't in the mood for the forced polite talk which always accompanies acquaintances rather than friends. I now just wanted to get thoroughly pissed and be able to tell people to fuck off without them taking offence. For me trailing through pubs looking for someone is alright just so long as it ends up being raucously inebriated amongst friends, otherwise you simply end up solemnly drunk with the feeling that everyone is busy avoiding you. Where the hell were they?

I exchanged pleasantries with the colleagues. After all, what else can you do? and told them I'd go on to the "Dschungel" and would maybe see them there later. I needed to get away and get some serious drink in. I'd had a sandwich for lunch and the lack of calories was making my head spin, but I knew if I stopped to eat I'd be out of time and out of cash. I said my farewells and stepped back out into the heat muffled street and made my sweaty way down to my next stop.

If the heat was heavy going outside the atmosphere which met me as I pulled open the Dschungel's heavy iron door was fucking gruelling. The blackened poster pasted walls sucked up the already dim light so I had to squint my eyes to see if they were there. 'Least it wasn't winter so I didn't have to go through the demeaning ritual of rubbing my sweating glasses on my dirty shirt sleeve, only to see them cloud over again and having to repeat the whole process. In winter I desperately try to avoid going into bars looking for people.

And there they were, huddled around their bottles and glasses at the back of the pub. They waved me over when they saw me through the gloom of the smoked out room, and, as soon as I'd got a beer bottle in my hand, I squeezed my way through the matt black painted stools toward them. We underwent the usual negotiations of exchanging greetings and organizing suitable seating for us all. This was, of course, totally unsuitable for me, since I ended up sitting on the end of a bench. This was next to Maria who was deeply engrossed in a gripping conversation with Marten, leaving me to admire the shade of black used to decorate the wall opposite.

They'd already been here an hour and were well tanked up, and the mood was good. But I felt like a lemming perched on the end of the bench waiting to jump off at the slightest provocation as their laughter rolled distantly through my slightly drunken head. I scratch the wax encrusted on the table with my hand, a miasma of beer dulled thoughts glazing my expression as the lively chatter entirely fails to animate me. Another pissed up night full of empty talk like the lines of empty bottles. Dumb and glum I think, as a heavy hand thumps me on the shoulder and I turn to look up at Kurt's slightly sheepish face. Perhaps it's the light, but he looks red and warm, swaying somewhat drunk with a pained grin on his face.

"Alright," I say, gesturing him to sit down at the table next to ours, smiling relieved at the prospect of a conversation which wouldn't reinforce me feeling like a lemming. First he lumbered over to the bar to get a drink, a "Hefeweißen," a strong yeasty brew which I myself am not fond of, but which Kurt can consume by the gallon.

Coming back he looks at me, shaking his head, "Shit, I think I made a mistake."

Apricot Juice and Other Stories...

"What's up, what you done now?" I ask, more interested in getting a stool than in his answer. Setting my lazy drunken backside down opposite him I try to fain enthusiasm for his dilemma. "C'mon tell me, whatchyou do?" but the glaze in his eyes tells me it isn't going to come out like that. With Kurt it never comes out like that, he needs a bit, does our Kurt.

He sups heavily at his beer, scratches at his nose, coughs, then peers at me through the gloom, shaking his head "Nichts, nichts."

"What's the problem then? You said something to Thorsten, or what?"

But he's looking at the others now, who've seen him, asking him how's it going, what's he doing. He waves his hand in the air, part as if he's royalty waving to the crowd, part to fend of the queries coming his way. "Ach Ja, fine fine, alles in Ordnung," he throws over to them in a tone so heavy you'd think Hamburg's homeless would all be sleeping at his place tonight. This is getting ridiculous.

"Kurt, what the fuck's up" I say as turns back to me, looking at me , then into his glass, scratches his nose again, then looks back at me. He sighs, I sigh, then I say, "OK, OK, nothing's up, you're fine, I'm fine, the world and his wife's fine."

He laughs, looking confused at my outburst, and says, "Yeah, no, I mean I don't know what I said, but Thorsten's...." he grunts, throwing his hands into the air, as if this will explain everything. Kurt is well known for giving his voice to his problems. After about

Apricot Juice and Other Stories...

five hours of interrogation, that is. He runs his hand through his curls and chuckles slyly to himself.

"You pissed?" I ask as if I didn't know.

"Totally. Nah, I'm not so bad, just a bit, that's all," he answers, but judging by the way he's looking it's a bit more than just a bit, but that's what we're here for anyway.

I ask "What's with Thorsten then? Wasn't he getting at you earlier? Looked like it any ways when I came in."

"No, not then, he was just bending my ear about some woman who he was waiting for. Nah, this was later, after you'd gone. He was steaming. I dunno, I guess I shouldn't have said anything." He takes a long swig at his beer, and then waves his large hand through the air as if to brush his troubles away like a fly. But I'm not having any of it. He can't just come in telling he's got troubles without going into the details, can he?

"What you say to him then? It can't be that bad. Come on Kurt, out with it," I say, imploring.

"Not to him, to her, to her. I shouldn't have said anything to her," he says as if I'm a spastic, but I'm well and truly lost now. The place's beginning to fill up now and my gaze falls away from Kurt's to wander over the newcomers. This particular bar attracts a particular kind of custom, best described as young, left-wing, slightly punky, football fans, St. Pauli of course. Except for the dominance of leather jackets there's no real regulation clothing here, so long as it's old, dark and preferably with lots of holes torn into it. Obligatory is unkempt hair of varying lengths and colours and the hurried consumption of a lot of alcohol. The atmosphere is loud and friendly. Remembering friends I turn back to try to concentrate on what Kurt's gabbling on about.

"He was going on about fancying this girl who was sitting at the bar. All he talks about nowadays is women. I reckon he's got a real problem with women, I mean, he runs after them like that's it for him, that's his life. I reckon he's got a real problem being alone, if you ask me. I just wanted to help out, but..."

I'm staring at him after this unusual little monologue, but I manage to say, "Yeah, but what the fuck happened, what exactly did you say?"

I mean, this was a reasonable request after all this build up, but he looks at me like I've squashed him in a corner with a gun against his head. He starts to raise his voice, but there's a truculent whine to it as he says, "I don't know, I don't remember, do I, but it was bad enough..."

"What you mean you don't fucking remember? Then it can't have been that bad. But you spoke to her, did you, then what about?" I ask.

But I lost him somewhere, he just goes on, "Man, he was mad afterward. I mean he was ranting, at the end we was both ranting at each other, right in the middle of the pub. I had to go, otherwise I'd 've hit him, or he'd 've landed one on me, that's why I came here, I can't take his bullshit anymore, but I don't think I said the right thing, like I only wanted to help out, but he didn't see it like that, he was steaming."

I try to intervene, "But what did you talk to her about? C'mon, you must remember something."

This time he hears me, and says, "Well, about him, like he was sitting there, he wasn't going to say anything and I thought, no, I didn't think, but..." then he stands up abruptly, asking, "you want another beer?" I nod my head and watch as he lurches over to the bar, wondering what the fuck could have got him so wound up. Trouble was he was pissed, but he didn't look that pissed that he couldn't remember what he said. That I couldn't believe. But it must have been pretty embarrassing to him, so I start making guesses as to what he might have said.

He comes back to the table, glass in one hand, a bottle for me in the other. Looking across at him with a smile on my face I say, "So what you do wrong, you didn't try and chat her up did you? I mean that'd be bad, him telling you that he likes her, and you moving straight in there."

He sighs heavily, a grimace tightening his slightly rounded features, and then rounds and straightens his shoulders as if he's just taken a blow and is preparing for more where that came from. He says, a bit sternly, "I'd never do that, who do I look like anyway?"

This was getting tiring, and I wasn't getting any more sober, and the acid's rising in my throat. I take another swig of my beer, which doesn't do anything for my stomach, but before I can say another word he blurts out with, "I think I told her that he fancies her."

Apricot Juice and Other Stories...

I'm nonplussed, "And?" I ask.

"That was all. I mean, I don't know exactly what I said, but something like that." He shakes his head and stares at the table as if he's guilty of a major crime.

"And I thought it was a major drama. I mean, alright, it's a bit embarrassing, but if she was into him then what's the problem, it don't matter what you say, it would've worked anyway. Or?" I'm beginning to get that sinking feeling which I often tend to get when talking with these people. I mean Kurt makes a great play of not saying anything as if he's said the worst thing in the world and seriously damaged his friend's pride. And what's it turn out to be, what'd he say, oh excuse me I think you should know that my friend fancies you. Yup, big problem, but in the head if you ask me. Why the fuck do they have to take every single little utterance to heart? Makes me positively nervous at times it does. But I always thought of Kurt as one of the straighter ones, which it turns out he is.

He takes me in with a long glazed look and says, "yeah, but Thorsten didn't see it that way. He thought I was interfering. He went berserk like I said. He starts shouting, the girl starts crying, it was a disaster."

Now it's my turn to shake my head. "I don't know, if you ask me that bloke's not right in his head. I mean alright, it's a bit of a pisser what you did, but it couldn't have done any real harm. You mean he started shouting at you just 'cos you said that he fancied her?"

He looks at me like some hunted animal as I

stare in disbelief thinking that it's a mad, mad world in which we find ourselves in, and answers, "That's what I'm telling you. We were both shouting, don't know what they thought of us in the pub. I was surprised they didn't throw us out."

I reached across the table and patted his arm, "Don't worry 'bout it, don't even think about it. I mean the man's not right in his head. Did I tell you I met him the other night?" He shakes his head, "On the Kietz. I mean it wasn't a bad night, but he was so fucking strung out, like he'd taken a packet of speed or something. And all he went on about was women. I mean like Lisa was there and he was asking me about the women there as if I could answer him in front of her. Martina and Michaela were there and they just wanted to get away and he was like...ah fuck it, don't worry about it, it's not the end of the world is it, he'll get over it." I hoped my monologue would be enough to soothe his nerves, I mean who wants to get pissed in the company of a guilt wracked wreck? Not me for one.

But it seems to do the trick. Kurt almost giggles as he says, "Thorsten's hardly got a world to end. That's his problem. All he's got is himself and his ego, and can't even deal with that. I mean he's always going on about me not having a girlfriend, but at least I can enjoy myself without running after women all the time. And he's got no respect for them, or for anyone else for that matter."

And so we plundered into one of those psychological slagging matches where you systematically and normally very drunkenly assassinate the fuck out of your closest friend's character. Not exactly what you call productive, but it beats the hell out of moaning about your own deficits, and makes you feel a fuck of a lot better about yourself. I always have to gasp in admiration at the gentle ways of human nature.

What comes out at the end of all this is what he actually said to the girl was not that Thorsten fancied her. Oh no, he goes and tells her that Thorsten's actually in love with her. Embarrassing, embarrassing, but what the hell, it's hardly the end of the world, is it?

That's what I'm thinking as a face tight with anger peers over Kurt's shoulder, a large hand on his shoulder. Fuck, it's Thorsten. Fuck, fuck. Normally in such situations a poignant silence might fall across the company, but this is Thorsten and he is definitely not normal.

He ploughs straight in, "Du verfickter Scheiß-kerl, just tell me one thing, one thing, why did you do it? C'mon tell me, why'd you do it?" He's continuously jabbing Kurt with his index finger like he's testing him for firmness, and I'm telling you, Kurt is not someone you need to test for firmness, not with your finger, not unless you're mad. Thorsten was fucking mad.

He grabs a stool from the table next to us, thumps it down, and turns his finger on me, "You stay here, I want you to hear this, 'cos for once I want someone else to hear what an arsehole he is, I want someone else to judge whether I'm being fair or not."

"OK," I say, thinking that this is not ok at all.

Apricot Juice and Other Stories...

Thorsten looks like someone's threaded a needle through the skin in the nape of his neck and is slowly pulling the thread tight. He's got his hair shorn fingernail short at the moment and I can see a vein pulsing on his temple. Never mind, maybe it'll fucking burst and we'll all be spared the effort. I definitely do not need this.

A bright idea pops into my head all at this moment. Offer him a drink I think. Try and get him to loosen up a bit, "I need a drink, Thorsten, you want a beer?" I ask, sliding of my perch, a sick kind of smile wallpapered across my mush. He looks at me like I just cleaned his shoes and used shit for shoe polish. I brace myself for another onslaught. Which comes like this:

"No, and you know why? 'Cos I'll end up pissed just like the rest of you fucking alcoholics here and that's not for me. I already had to knock back a couple of shorts just to steady my nerves after what this cunt did." He jerks his head at Kurt, and carries on impervious to the way Kurt's staring at him like some kind of cartoon character with his eyes popping out on their stalks and his jaw dropping down to his feet. "I'm not going to end up like him with his brain soused in fucking beer," he turns to Kurt without taking a breath, "just tell me one thing, one thing, what you do it for?" Then he turns back to me and says "I'll have a' apricot juice thanks."

So I trundle off, making my way to the bar as quick as poss, thinking "he wants a fucking apricot juice, who the fuck drinks fucking apricot juice at a time like this, or even ever?" The words apricot juice, "Aprikosen Saft," stick in my head, painted in their sick dripping orange colour, revolving around as if they were some sort of surreal neon sign, advertising things to come. I fucking hate apricot juice.

I grab the hated drink and my beloved beer from the bar girl, not failing to notice how the many rings on her chubby fingers reflect the noxious hue emanating from the glass. Hastily I thrust a note into the same hand saying, "that's alright," but she doesn't understand and turns back to give me the change which she should-'ve kept. There's a hammer going in my head playing a staccato to the rhythm of Thorsten's anger and the colour of apricot juice, so I just snatch it off her and don't say a word, which really isn't like me at all, and march back to the table thumping the drinks down. Then grabbing a beer mat I try and stop the spilt beer running off the table onto my trousers. I'm not feeling good at all.

Thorsten's berating Kurt in tones of ever increasing volume and takes the apricot juice which is now glowing dangerously in the ultraviolet strip lighting above our heads. He makes a jabbing sip at the liquid, which he then sprays in Kurt's direction in a small explosion of anguished hurt "you couldn't even say sorry you arsehole."

Kurt looks up, immediately blurting out an apology "I'm sorry, believe me I'm sorry I ever opened my mouth." But it doesn't seem to come out right because Thorsten face curls up in a triumphant sneer as if Kurt's apology justifies him thinking that he's a worthless shit.

"But you can't tell me why you did it, can you? That's all I want to hear, I just want to understand why you think it's your right to get mixed up in my business. C'mon, tell me, why'd you have to speak to her, what made you think that it was your place to move in there?" He would've gone on but one of the women next to him turns and taps him on the shoulder. He spins round his face tight and shiny with aggression, and growls "what you want?"

"I want to drink my drink in peace. We just got back from work and we all want to just sit and have a quiet drink and a chat, but I can't hear what the others are saying because you're shouting in my ear all the time."

The quietly controlled modulations of suppressed righteous anger which characterise the social worker in action have absolutely no effect on Thorsten as he blithely answers, "Well fuck off and go somewhere else then. I mean, where do you think you are, in your fucking living room? This is a pub. This is my table, that's your table, we're having a conversation, you're having a conversation, and there's no reason for us to be having a conversation together, because if you think I'm talking too loud then you can find yourself another fucking table or another fucking pub. Is that understood? "

She looks at him like he's clinically insane, which at this moment he probably is, takes a deep breath and starts again, "Look, we'd just appreciate it if you could be a little quieter..."

He shakes his head vigorously, "I mean, do you understand what I'm saying? I am sitting at my table having a conversation which has absolutely nothing to do with you at all, and I will speak exactly as loud as I please and say what I fucking want to. If you don't like either then find somewhere else to drink. Is this clear to you? Do...you...understand?"

To give her her due, despite being a rather diminutive five foot tall or small, this outrageous outburst did nothing to intimidate her. Tossing her black hair back as if she were some kind of movie starlet she eyes him up and down as if he were a cockroach crawled out from under her brand sparkling new Siemens' fridge freezer. Then she says, "Look, it's not me who's having problems understanding things, but you probably won't understand that either, but please, please, just keep it down will you?" and without waiting to see how he'd react, turns back to her mates, her dark eyes rolling backwards in their sockets.

Thwarted in his tracks Thorsten takes up the attack on the home front. With eyes like an offshore drilling platform he stares at Kurt and jerks his thumb over his shoulder towards where the others are sitting, and sneers "that's why you ran off and came here wasn't it? You couldn't face me alone could you, you fucking coward. You had to come here to your fucking little nest of alcoholics you call friends."

I see Kurt rising to the bait, his fists balling on

the table, so I step in, or leastways try to step in, saying "Hold on a mo' Thorsten, you're not giving the guy a chance..."

But that's all I get out with, he turns on me his eyes blazing, "you shut it, you got no business saying anything, this is between me and him..." I open my mouth like a gold fish to try again, but to no avail. He wags his finger at me and snaps, "I said shut it, not another word, hear?"

Kurt sees his moment and jumps right in, "that's you're problem isn't it," he says, "you don't even want to listen to what someone else wants to say, you haven't given me a chance to say anything and now you turn on him, I mean you asked him earlier to say what he thought, and now he's got to fucking shut up."

Thorsten's straight back in there, in the breath which Kurt has to draw, "See, you don't like it, someone taking over, do you? So why'd you fucking do it? Did you give me a chance to speak did you? No. And that was my fucking film. You understand? You didn't belong in it. Had absolutely fucking nothing to do with you, that was my fucking game and you showed no fucking respect, just barged in there, and then you fuck off to your fucking alkie friends. Maybe that's alright for them," he sneers at the group, "they probably don't know any better. But it's not good enough for me. You understand that. Do you get it that I'm an individual and got a right to my own life without some fucking soused idiot sticking his fucking nose in it and showing me no respect?..."

Apricot Juice and Other Stories...

And so he goes on. And on. And on. And fucking on. My hand's on the neck of my beer bottle and I'm wondering whether the bottom of it pasted across Thorsten's forehead would constitute modern art or causing an affray when my troubled gaze alights upon the ominously glowing apricot juice. My teeth are grinding and muscles aching due to prolonged exposure to violent ranting. Then my mind dislocates itself from all sense of responsibility as I watch my hand reaching towards the book of matches lying next to the infamous drink and flicking the glass lightly so it tumbles, odious contents and all, over Thorsten's pressed white chinos.

This is possibly the stupidest and bravest act I've committed in the last ten years. Brain flips into overdrive, amazed at what my body has just done, and hoping to god that it works. "Sorrysorrysorry" streams from my lips directed at Thorsten, "gohomefuckoff-gohome" races through my head and the adrenaline hits my stomach as I brace myself for the inevitable. And then total unbelievable shut down. The cunt isn't even fazed. He doesn't even wipe his trousers. He just carries on haranguing Kurt. As I said, apricot juice does nothing for me.

I am now just a reeling yo-yo as I hear him, his voice a blunt knife digging painful holes in Kurt's psyche. Kurt's given up even with pretence of defending himself, "Look Thorsten, there's no point talking with you now about this. I've had enough now, you've insulted me, you insulted my friends, so lets just leave it alright? I just want to drink the rest of my beer in peace."

And I just want to go home now as Thorsten starts again with "Who are your friends then Kurt? Tell me that at least. I was supposed to be your fucking friend, but if you prefer these inarticulate slags to me, then just say the word and we can forget our friendship, you think I'm scared of you, just 'cos of your size, fuck you I can take you any day you cunt..." but Kurt was already on his feet now, reaching for Thorsten, as I hang onto the table to try and stop it falling over.

"That's it, that's enough, you come in here, you insult me, I care about that, but you have to push it, you have to insult my friends..." and he grabs Thorsten by the buckle on his belt and lifts him off the stool so he's dangling there horizontal shouting "fuck off you cunt, get off me," and waving his arms and legs about as Kurt tries to carry him like this to the door, but stumbles over Thorsten's windmilling legs so they both fall in a heap of outstretched limbs, and everyone's getting up now and moving towards the two with shouts of "Hey, hey," and "hoi, hoi," and I see Kurt coming to a stand, still trying to pick Thorsten up to throw him out, when Thorsten's fist shoots out, his arm straight, and there's a smack of flesh as it connects soundly with Kurt's cheek, but his head hardly moves as he hauls Thorsten to his feet and throws him in amongst the tables and stools, and then there's all of us with our hey heys and hoi hois, about ten of us all trying to grab a piece of the action as we hang on to a tee-shirt or a leg or an arm of one or the other, except Michaela who's got hold of Martin who's being wheeled around by Thorsten so that I see the bemused look on her face as she swings past me tottering to the other side of the pub, and then I get my bit of action as I feel Thorsten's arm in my hand, slip my arm up to his elbow and twist his wrist up behind his back, pulling him away from Kurt, till he wrenches himself around, fist raised, and I cower behind my spindly arms thinking "fuck I'm going to die."

And then it stops. Thorsten doesn't hit me and there's a chorus of go homes and get outs as he's ushered out the door by us ten deputies, and the door's locked behind him and there's a lot of shaking heads and muttered "nutter," and "idiot," and "you alright?" and "is he gone?"

I turn round to Kurt, noting the swelling on his cheek, it's cut as well, and he's saying "let me out, I'm going to finish the bastard..." and everyone else making conciliatory cooing noises "it's not worth it," "leave it," "sit down," "drink your beer."

But Kurt's not having any of it and marches toward the door. I try and bar his way by grabbing his hand and twisting his finger, but he just laughs at me and takes his hand back and says, "I'm going to finish him once and for all," and tries the door but it's locked so he turns to the barmaid, "let me out." Fearing for the door which he's rattling to a dangerous degree she does so, and I follow him out into the night.

We're standing there, and the rain's coming down, and we can't see Thorsten. I turn to Kurt, saying, "come on let's go back in, come and sit with your friends," but he's sobbing now, his body heaving with the effort, the tears falling freely. I put an arm on his shoulder, "c'mon mate, it's not so bad, come inside..." but he brushes it away.

"I got no friends anymore, twenty years I knew that guy, twenty fucking years we were friends, he was the last one, now he's gone like the rest of them. I'm alone here, just fucking alone." He wipes a heavy hand across his eyes. Suddenly, from behind, a voice cuts through the rain. It's Thorsten.

"Nick, come here, I've got to talk to someone. Please. I just got to talk to talk with someone." His voice is cracked like he's crying too, but I can't face him, not again, "Piss off Thorsten, just fuck off, go home," I start yelling down the road at him, and watch as he gets on his bike and starts to ride off, his head bobbing smaller and smaller as he pumps at the pedals to put some distance between him and this night. I turn round and watch as Kurt heads off in the other direction, snuffling and then stopping, mindlessly kicking at a car door, then moving off again, erratically zigzagging across the road, his body slowly melting into the darkness, leaving me alone with the rain and the night.

.

A RUN IN WITH THE LAW

Kaleidoscope colours and washing room smells afflict, conflict, corrupt and almost DUPE his senses, like an old sixties Motown song, doo doo do de do de do doo doo, serenading you into another world of beautiful HOT women with smooth dudes and long cars. Al swings his black leather holdall up from the clanking conveyor, letting it slap against his shoulder with a satisfying thud. Meanwhile he's shooting a sly, but obviously SCINTILLATING, smile towards the one with the cat green eyes and a nose with such a sweet little curl it makes his eyes water and his groin tingle. Looking around the baggage claim hall for the way out he starts humming quietly to himself, thinking -

IT'S A HOLIDAY IN HAMBURG,
A HOLIDAY WITH THE HUN

but the words don't fit the music, so he gives it up and makes his way to the exit, picking green although he should take blue 'cos he's a European just like you and I.

The German customs, however, no doubt due to their hermetically sealed upbringing in a monolithic WHITE society whose borders they are committed to SERVE and PROTECT, don't quite see it that way. In their monogamous language, any shade darker than pale, pallid or pink signifies DRUGS, DIRT, DISEASE and DEATH, not to mention cheap labour.

So, as he saunters along, feeling good and

pleased with generally everything, trying to make out if Nick was already there among the waiting crowd behind the sliding doors, one of the blue suited gentlemen tugs at his cap, and beckons Al over with a crooked finger and a yellow toothed smile. A green suited policeman comes to his aid, with his hand on his pistol, maybe just to check that it's there, then again, maybe not. Together they lead Al into a small brightly lit office behind all the desks where you normally empty your bags. And all he's thinking is "Aw, fer fuck's sake man, why me," knowing full well he should've bleached his skin before making this particular trip.

"Watch you takin' me in here for?" he asks, trying to sound aggrieved, but inside he's shitting himself. This is not because he's carrying anything, but because you'd be shitting it too if two armed gentlemen, one with a large baton secreted away in a hidden trouser pocket, asked you to accompany them alone into a brightly lit room.

The room's not really a room, but a small Formica cubicle, about eight foot square, making it more than a bit crowded when the three of them crowd in there. Al's sweating like a clammy fish, and feels his belly doing gyrations for which it was not designed. In front of him there's an olive green coloured desk, matching the olive green coloured wall onto which it's fixed, which all in all served to produce a sickly feeling which it was obviously intended to do. Al accordingly felt sick and then remembered that this might have something to do with the fact that the claustrophobic cubicle, together with two armed uniformed men, had made him forget to breathe. Glancing round he lets out a lungful of air with a sigh he knows sounds suspect.

The customs' man stares at him out of old rheumy eyes blinking behind a pair of thick lensed, heavy rimmed, rectangular shaped glasses. If he hadn't had that dumb cut and hang of the uniformed man he could have been a middle aged lecturer who'd liberally fight for the undernourished rights of Al's pigmentation, but he wasn't. What he was, was a cunt, and it shows in his dead eyed smile as he motions Al to put his bag on the table and takes out a Stanley knife with its blue-grey gun metal case and single sharp metallic tooth, and lays it down beside the bag.

Dipping a liver flecked hand in like a magician going into his box of tricks, with a weird performing smile cracking his lips, he pulls out the plastic bag with Al's NIKES in it. Like a frightened chameleon trying to fit into its surrounds Al blanches when he sees the thin peel of black rubber as the keen little blade slices into the sole. FORTYNINENINETYFIVE, FORTYNINE-NINETYFIVE, goes through his head 'cos he knows he'll not get them at that price again. Our friend and helper, the customs man, twists back the flapping sole to reveal the neatly cut air pockets which give the shoe its famous cushioned bounce, helping world class athletes to leap extremely tall buildings and young teenagers to mug extremely old people. Al feels even SICKER.

But today that little trickle of whitish powder, which would've given the game away had Al been a DANGEROUS DRUG DEALER, is not trickling. Not from the first shoe, not from the second. Disgusted, the man in blue throws them to the floor, picks up the holdall, turns it upside down, and lets the content cascade over the table, the camera spilling brokenly onto the floor. Al feels his throat constrict, and an angry tear prick at his eyeball, as he thinks of all the things he's not got, like insurance, a lawyer, an uzzi. "C'mon guy, be careful wiv my stuff, like whose goin' to pay for that camera there?"

He points a limp hand at the busted camera, thinking about how Marlene was going to lynch him. She'd saved for it a long time, months, really fucking saved like he'd never done. He always took credit; 'cept he couldn't get none anymore, but she couldn't handle that, everything was bought cash, or she'd not buy it. She was sound but she'd said "Al, you bust my camera, don't bother comin' back." TWOHUNDREDAND-FIFTYFUCKINGQUID, where was he going to get TWOHUNDREDANDFIFTYFUCKINGQUID? But there's only questions, and no answer from his tormen-tor.

His back was river wet now. He shoots a despairing glance at the greened policeman as the other man picks up the camera, looks him in the eye, smiles like a fish, and drops it on the floor again. Al should've known better. Greeny starts awhistling, his eyes rolling toward the ceiling. Al's stomach takes another turn, but this time there's a painful pressure in his belly which he suddenly realizes is not due to his existential angst. The desperation evident in his eyes and the squirm in his buttocks indicates to the sharp eyed customs man that it's all up his ARSE.

His eyes take on a wicked glint, and his smile becomes a satisfied sneer as he turns his attention to the man himself. Al's eyes widen to bulging orbs as he sees the walrus fatted man take a white powered plastic glove and pull it onto his right hand with a sharp little snap. The custom's man tells Al to remove his trousers and underpants and to bend down please. For once in his life Al thinks of the words in the bible - THEY KNOW NOT WHAT THEY DO! He starts to plead, "hey, c'mon don't do this, I'm a Muslim, this is strictly against my religion," but to no avail as greeny moves with a threatening hand on a glistening pistol toward him.

He nearly doubles over as a needle pang of pain hits his bowels, but turns around, face agrimace, pulling hastily at his buckled belt. Pulling down his pants he bends down to place his little brown arsehole right in the face of the man in blue, who takes his rubbered finger and sticks it roughly right up his by now burning hole and rudely wiggles it around. The bile starts to climb Al's throat as he feels the strange pressure at the base of his cock. He grits his teeth, grinding them 'til his fillings threaten crack as the chuckling fat walrus keeps his finger wriggling, and his cocks' gone hard, about to explode, when his bowels grumble with a final painful wave, and, with a gut heaving stink, spray yellow brown clinging liquid fetid shit into the retching face of the man from customs.

Al starts vomiting as the stench hits the back of his nose, and he hears the two men busy at their noisy barfing. Laughter shakes his already heaving body as he raises his head, his hands pressing against his knees, to see the blinding iron blow of the policeman's pistol as it cracks across the base of his skull. Our hero's last thought before he loses consciousness? I REALLY FUCKING SHAT ON THEM!

DISINFECTANTS AND OTHER IRRITATING THINGS

Nick couldn't remember exactly why he used to be so open and enthusiastic towards the clients he met at work. Perhaps, in those early days, he had just been naive. But he remembered precisely the day on which his enthusiasm had died. He sucked damply on his cigarette, letting the smoke snake lazily from his nostrils, until the wandering snake turned and bit him sharply, causing him to sneeze. He hacked out a cough, the squeeze of a tear rolling sympathetically out of the corner of his eye and down the side of his face. But he wasn't crying. He was seething. He took a huge gulp of the warming beer from the large chunky glass, it had been standing too long in the bright sun, and squinted from the pub's metal fenced terrace across the square toward the entrance to the drugs unit, his current place of employment. He raised his glass in a sardonic salute to the building and swilled the remaining contents down his throat. He'd just had another bloody stupid argument with one of his bosses who just happened to be a friend. In this place it was a case of too many social workers and not enough cleaners, he thought to himself.

Her perfume still hung sharply in his nose. He could still feel the wash of her breath on his face from when she had shouted at him, a moment ago, her eyes drilling into his, her nose quivering a few inches away from his. He could still see her as she strode angrily away towards the main station. He thought that she was probably crying. He'd wanted to take her head in his hands and to kiss her while she'd been shouting at him. He couldn't remember what she'd said exactly, the same as she'd said before, except this time it had been noticeably louder. He'd switched off as soon as she'd started getting angry. He'd listened to the rising hysterical whine in her voice, concentrated on the cracks and the pucker of her slightly dry lips thickly rimming her small mouth, watched as her lucid eyes moistened, the translucent tears slowly welling up. He'd expected her to stomp her feet as she'd dramatically risen to leave, shouting at him that he was impossible.

Nick chewed on his lower lip, stabbed the cigarette out in the large metal ashtray, and raised his hand to attract the waiter's attention. The waiter was as pale as a junkie, with lank black hair parted in the middle and hanging greasily down both sides of his face. His chin was bonily pointed, his nose a large hook. He saw Nick waving at him through his dark eyes, ignored him entirely, and turned quickly and entered the door of the café. Nick muttered "Bitch" to himself, deciding it was better to blame Connie for the waiter's ignorance rather than the waiter himself since he would be needing him soon. He stood up and followed the bony young man into the musty darkness of the café, his sun squinted eyes almost blind in the gloom. It suited his mood.

He approached the wide bar, decked with a set of four brass beer taps, and ordered another beer, indicating the booth he was going to occupy to the man pulling the beer behind the bar. The waiter looked over at him and raised his nose haughtily as if Nick's decision to drink inside was a personal insult. As he walked stiffly over to Nick's booth Nick could see him in his mind's eye goosestepping, hand held high. The image caused him to smile madly at the young man, which no doubt only served to make him feel all the more irritated with Nick. He slapped his black purse down on the table and asked Nick to pay. Nick looked up at him, confusion almost crossing his eyes. He thought he was being thrown out. The waiter rubbed his long nose with two slender fingers and explained in an exasperated tone that he took care of the guests outside while the barman took care of the guests inside. Nick looked around, but there was no-one there. As he pulled at the change in his jeans' pocket he wondered abstractedly why the waiter was so annoyed at him since it was full outside anyway. He mentally shrugged his shoulders, thinking that it was probably down to the heat but decided to take it personally and not give the sultry bastard a tip. He resumed his mad smile as he pressed a single shiny five mark piece into the waiter's sweaty palm. He looked away in order to avoid the inevitable stony glare and waited patiently until the waiter had taken his leave. He looked up gratefully as the barman, following on the heels of the waiter, handed him his weighty glass of beer.

Nick took a hungry bite at the beer glass, downing almost half of its glinting liquid. As the cool gloom and the muffled wave of alcohol passed over him he became despondent. What right did she have to accuse him of not caring about the junkies? Who was she to say what he thought and felt? He took another swig of beer and in a haze of cynicism thought that the problem was that she was absolutely right. He knew that lately he'd distanced himself from the clients, that he'd developed certain defences against them. He no longer found their stories interesting, they were just the usual junkie palaver. He no longer forgave their aggressiveness and rudeness by assigning them to the raw drive of their addiction, but thought of them as being ignorant and violent. He still talked with them, asking this or that, sometimes engaging in small talk, sometimes being drawn into the long, meandering histories which were opened out before him, but felt his replies to be routine and hollow.

Only last week he'd sat there, sipping at a cup of coffee, absentmindedly listening to a junkie threatening to commit suicide. No-one else was about so Nick couldn't leave, but neither was he exactly there. He'd gone through the motions. He'd asked questions, listened to the man talking, emphasised any positive aspects of the man's story, told a few little anecdotes, either about himself, or about other junkies he'd known, in an effort to provide the man with a perspective, but he didn't engage. It wasn't that he didn't believe what the man was saying, he'd tried to kill himself last week. Nick just didn't particularly care whether the man died or not. He hadn't seen the man's pain, but he'd seen his wretched clothes, the swollen track marks on his neck, his bloated hands, his drug dulled eyes. He'd placed him in a group, named him a junkie, and saved himself the trouble of treating him as a person. He went through the motions and it had worked.

Nick looked up at the ceiling as the pictures rolled into his head. He watched the slow twist of the fan spinning above his head, the images in his head glancing of its flat blades. The anger rose hotly in his throat. Through its red gash we can think his thoughts.

- The fucking manky two faced bitch. Sitting there on her fucking stool telling me about who cares as if she gives a fuck for anything beyond her fucking pretty little nose. I got no experience, I don't know what I'm talking about? What's she seen in her fucking shitty little life. Fuck. Three o' clock and I'm pissed again. Fuck. But she's not seen what I saw. -

Suddenly the bright pictures were there again as he sped back to the time when junkies were people, people who connected, who were witty, sad, angry and not just stoned. André wandered into his revery, his eyes dancing sharply in his wide angular face. He'd always rushed out on seeing Nick, grabbing him by the arm, urging him to play just one quick game of table football. He was good but Nick was better and always won. André would laugh and with a friendly shrug he'd put it down to being stoned and demand an unachievable revenge. Or they'd sit in the office and chatter about their lives, about politics - André used to be a neo-Nazi before he took heroin, and then he stopped being a neo-Nazi and became a junkie. And he was a boxer before he became a neo-Nazi until he got into a street brawl and had to give up being a boxer and became a neo-Nazi.

They would talk about drinking, about drugs, about clubs but never about women. Nick never talked to men about women. André just never talked about women. André was a big man, the kind of man people used to call a bear of a man, or attribute with the constitution of an ox. He would drink a bottle of vodka every day, would take six or seven shots of H everyday, and Nick had often helped to lift the heavy man into bed after he'd slumped to the ground in the shower or lay sprawled across the desk in the office. But they'd never had to call the ambulance. He had a thick crop of mouse brown hair which he'd spike up with gel. He walked with a slight limp because he had a hole in his backside where they'd recently gouged out an abscess from one of his buttocks.

Nick had known about the abscess because one day, in fit of self righteous rage, André had pulled down his trousers to show one of the social workers just how bad his abscess was. Nick had been sitting in the office at the time, drinking a cup of coffee and eating a doughnut. Nick had already taken a bite out of the doughnut and couldn't help associating the oozing jam with Andrés' abscess. It didn't stop him finishing the doughnut, he loved doughnuts. And Nick had liked André.

Nick returned from his revery and looked about him. Next to his high walled booth, fashioned with a dark oak veneer, was a table made of a large black wooden water barrel. Atop this barrel stood a bronze statue of a man hewing a rock with a pick. Since beginning his job as a cleaner Nick identified fully with this image of the worker at work although it was seldom that he was to be found actually working. Staring sourly at the man he began reconstructing the day he stopped really liking André. As was his wont when angry, he began an internal monologue, as if he were telepathically telling the statue his story.

I know on the day I had a blinder of a hangover, trying to wash the dirt from the dirt coloured tiles and feeling sick as a dog, the yellow white bile biting the back of my throat. Swabbing the mop from side to side, which does your back in, splashing brown water over the brown tiles, I was waiting for the aspirin to take effect. I was in a bad state as André came into the café, a wolfish smile hanging from his lips. His whole body sagged as he slouched towards me, nodding with his head at the kicker table. I leant on the metal handled mop for much needed support, and rubbed my sweaty forehead across the sleeve of my sweat damp tee-shirt. I was in no state to play football. And that was even if André was swaying stoned on his feet. I felt like he looked but there was no way that either of us would back down from our daily game.

We both moved over to the table, I kept an eye on André to make sure he wasn't about to collapse and grabbed the plastic handles to the kicker table, spinning them once or twice to see how sticky they were today. André did likewise, but you could see that his level of concentration wouldn't be up to much. How could you see it? By the way he kept swaying over the table, his eyes half lidded. He'd do this everyday. Go out at nights, come in for breakfast, take his first shot, and then try and stay awake. Eventually he would crash for a couple of hours, and then take the next shot. The he'd down a bottle of Voddy.. I didn't want to think about his liver. Or his kidneys. Or his brain for that matter. Nice bloke though. Fucking stupid junkie.

Nick looked up, his monologue soured by the cascade of fury rushing over him. He let his gaze wander, as if it would allow his indignation to seep away into the scenery. He tried to think back to his monologue, this time attempting to perceive André's perspective. He found himself looking at himself through what he thought were drug shot eyes, his flimmering features wavering in and out of focus. He saw the ball rolling and his hands moving and felt his body swaying, but he was somewhere else. He saw Nick in front of him, practically twitching with a wild neurotic nervousness, he didn't know how Nick could cope with it, it looked like he was being physically peeked with needles of worry instead of needles of heroin. With a lurch André realised that Nick's last twitch had just won him the game. He smiled sloppily because he couldn't help it, not because he particularly wanted to. He smiled again as Nick grabbed at his slop mop and slouched off to wash the floor. What was wrong with being a junk?

Crap, thought Nick. Pure adolescent idealising romanticising crap. Give the cunt a month he wouldn't even remember my bloody name he was so screwed up.

Maybe in another life, but not one we can give him. His life is drugs - drugs high and drugs want, the unbroken cycle of pure supply and demand, the perfection of a means-end rationality, what the fuck are we going to teach that boy about modern life that he don't already know? And the fucker's seen more pure happiness than any of us, that's his problem.

Where was I? Right, right. We finished the game, and I watched him leaning over the table, smiling stupidly at my win. It was no contest, never was, 'cept when he was straight, then the gormless bastard would whup the fucking arse off me. 'Course, that wasn't often was it? Pity, it was nice to have a good game now and then, keeps the reflexes up. I'm sweeping the floor now. Don't swing the broom from left to right, just back and forwards, otherwise it does your back in. Look at the fucker, he can hardly stand. You can see him literally melting in and out of consciousness, slumping floorwards just to pick himself up before it's too late.

I don't remember what day it was, only what happened, the name of the day wasn't really important. Let's call it Wednesday for arguments sake. It was hot. It got really hot in there, 'specially when you were moving, then the sweat would run rivers off you. Since I was the only one who really had to move, 'cept when they had a load of fresh syringes in, I was the only one who really sweated, and they used to look at me like I was an alien or ill or something. It was only the junks who knew why I was sweating, but generally they didn't give a toss either.

André did, though, as much as he could, anyway. I once caught him and...what was his name?.. Jenz, Jenz is clean now, but they were both sitting in the office - the guy on duty had gone shopping - smiles as sweet as could be plastered on their faces as they sat there dragging on a long pipe of grass, the small room filled with the heavy smelling smoke. André offered me the pipe as I stumbled in wide eyed, he knew I enjoyed a puff now and then, but I had to refuse - you didn't know whether they had hepatitis or not and I hadn't had my jabs.

But that wasn't the only reason, of course. One was the heavy dose of paranoia I knew I'd get as soon as walked passed a social worker. But the most important was reason the fear that then they'd have something on you, the junks I mean, and there was never any doubt in my mind that if they had to they'd use it against you. I wasn't up for that. André saw that straight away, shook his head, and took a big black lump of shit out of his pocket and stuck it in my glove. I was about to give it back, he held up his hand in a warning gesture and said, "Listen, take it, there's no obligation. If Jenz or me tries to use that against you all you got to do is say you never got anything. Who're they going to believe? A couple of conniving junkies or their trusted caretaker?" I took the lump out my glove and regretfully pressed it back into his hand with a rueful smile. "They're social workers mate. They'll always put the word of a junkie above that of their trusted caretaker, believe you me." He laughed sardonically and pocketed the lump deftly, the quick movements of his thick fingers betraying the practised habit of secreting small packages about his body.

That was earlier though. Not on this Wednesday when he lumbered back to his room, giving me a shoulder jarring slap as passed by, already eager for his next shot.

The natural pause in Nick's story nicely fitted in with his emptied beer glass. He contemplated it wistfully, stroking the top of the glass slowly with forefinger and thumb, tipping it this way and that, letting the dregs slop from side to side. He held the glass up to face and nodded decisively to himself. He turned his head to try and catch the bony waiter's eye.

He felt his stomach growl and remembered that he hadn't yet eaten. The waiter saw him looking and turned obstinately away. Nick smiled sardonically and stretched a shaky hand out for the brown plastic menu, even though he already knew what he was going to eat. But such is the power of choice that he thought it only fair to see whether he might want something else today. Having given the choice more than a fair chance he chose what he always ate, a Monsieur Croque consisting of two thick sticks of toasted bread running over with a heavy melted cheese in which chunks of ham and pineapple swum. Nick could already feel his mouth watering as he turned round once more to try and catch the elusive waiter's eye, this time not by looking but by provocatively clicking his fingers. He smiled as charmingly as possible as the waiter marched over to him, a thick browed menace glowering in his face.

Nick suddenly broke out in sweated confusion as the long man leant over him and hissed in his ear that he'd already said that he was not responsible for taking the orders inside and that if Nick wanted to lose his fat arse he could either exercise it in the direction of the bar or in the direction of the door. Nick flushed at the latent violence whispering in the man's voice and the thought that he might have a fat arse. He stared at the table, fiercely avoiding the look and grabbing at the table edge as if the man had been one of his old school teachers. The waiter, having made his point, swept out of the door with his haughty high stepped walk , feeling the cold trickle running down his neck and relieved that that was the only consequence of his outburst. Nick looked bigger than he himself thought.

His face still a red bloom Nick stiffly unfolded himself up from the bench and walked slowly to the bar. The barman chuckled a little smile at him. Not wanting to upset the barman as well, he attempted a wan smile back, but he felt his lips quavering and hurriedly poured out his order to the grinning man. Nick turned abruptly away and slid himself back into his booth. He picked up the newspaper lying next to him and gazed at the black smudge of its text, too distracted to concentrate on their meaning. He sat there staring, not wanting to think, until the barman coughed politely by his side, a steaming plate in one hand, and a large glass in the other. "Baguette and beer," he said sharply, clacking them both loudly down onto the table.

Nick looked up and nodded his head in thanks.

Without thinking about the possible consequences Nick snatched a large bite out of the hot baguette and immediately began to suffer as the still simmering cheese began to blister the roof of his mouth. Gasping and chomping madly, his glasses steaming over as his face began to sweat, he grabbed for the cold beer, filling his mouth with the cooling liquid, swilling the flotsam of his food around until he was able to swallow it without major damage.

Having survived this minor crisis he slumped forward over the table, testing his smarting palate first with his tongue and then with his upturned thumb. He could feel a small balloon of flesh where the heat had caused the flesh to blister and scratched at it tentatively with his thumbnail. He felt the small fold of skin tear easily away and roll into a small sliver of flesh which he carefully pushed to the front of his mouth and out between his thumb and forefinger. He inspected it cursorily and flicked it away, annoyed that he had been so clumsy. He touched the bared, sore palate again to see whether it was bleeding. Satisfied that it wasn't he took another noisy slurp of beer and swilled it once more around his mouth, looking slyly around to catch the eye of any silent witness. The barman chuckled at him, saying, "Uhh, it's hot," and looked back down at the beer he was busy pulling. Nick swore under his breath, picked up the offending baguette and blew on the bitten end, testing it carefully with the tip of his tongue, which he also promptly burnt. He placed the baguette warily back onto its plate and took yet another swig of beer, aware that if he did not eat soon that not only would his mood would be so bad that no amount of sugar in his blood would assuage it but that he would be too drunk to enjoy his evening. He stared at the baguette accusingly and decided to set siege until its choleric heat had died down.

The anger growling in his empty stomach drove his thoughts snatching back to the unit. There were no more clever narratives now, simply a riven incense at which he grit his teeth. "Fucking dumb junkie cunt," he muttered to himself as the scenes flew at him. He felt the pulsing headache he'd had as André had stood swaying before him, an irritatingly lopsided smile smeared across his thickset features as if he'd just been to the dentist, his arms bear hugged around him as he started to shiver, apologizing that he had to go now, then looking back at Nick and offering a gritty laugh, "Fuck, you look worse than I feel, take a break mate. Got to fly." And with that he lumbered of along the corridor to his room.

Nick didn't remember the way the white tiles shouted blindingly in his face as he scrubbed away at the small drops of dried blood in the showers, or the way the matted clumps of hair hung onto the sink drains like wiry men clinging to a precipice as he pulled them away. He didn't remember rubbing at the chrome drains until they shone, coughing at the disinfectant he sprayed over the smooth surfaces, screwing up his eyes at the smell and at the ache in his head and hands. Nor did he remember dragging the wide broom along the over lit corridor from which the two toilets and two showers which he had to clean three dismal times a week, it's path picking up a small mound of crumbs, tobacco flakes and butt ends all tangled in an ever growing knot of ever present hair. The corridor led onto another, set at right angles to it, from which six rooms bled off. One was a sick room, one an office, the other bedrooms, each sleeping either two or three clients who were assigned them for up to two months - a respite where they could eat, sleep, wash and clothe themselves, all of them fucked to varying degrees and who left their rooms accordingly. If they were sick like André they could stay in during the day, although it was hard to tell who was sick and who not, those who weren't had to lock up their stuff and make it through the day outside until eight in the evening. Nick remembered none of this as he sat there wallowing in his drunken, indignant self-pity.

All he remembered was the white door in front of him at which he carefully knocked and listened. He remembered hearing André's gruff voice but not the words because hadn't heard what the man had said. He'd thought he'd said 'come in' and pushed the door open, lurching into the narrow room filled with its two beds and green painted steel lockup cabinets, seeing André lying stretched out, wide eyed and furious on the bed, his one grubby hand holding his engorged erect penis, in the other a muddy coloured syringe, its tip wavering in the air, an arc of brilliant blood spurting from the vein on André's penis where the needle had slipped out in surprise. "Get out!" he'd shouted, and sickened, Nick had stumbled backward out of the room.

He grasped at the wall, not feeling faint, but feeling that this was the appropriate reaction to what he'd just seen. Neither did he feel physically sick, but the gorge still rose in his throat. What he'd seen wasn't, in comparison to many of the things he'd seen at work, particularly shocking, but he was gut deep shocked, his face and hands white and cold, a thin bitter sweat coating his whole body, the hysterical scream of a small child roaring in his head.

He took a bite at his now cooled baguette and remembered walking shakily back across the café to sit down bemused in the conference room, staring blankly out at the junkies milling around outside, shouting, pushing, laughing and he recoiled. He remembered gathering himself together, walking back through the unit to the office where André was now standing, talking to a social worker, Detlef. Detlef looked embarrassed, and Nick could see why as André stood there in white underpants, turning to him, a pleading look of fearful chagrin pulling at his eyes, "I'm sorry, I didn't want you to see that, that was all," he said in stoned tones as two small rivulets of blood ran down each leg, drying as they went. Nick remembered looking at him and no longer seeing him, saying it was alright when it wasn't, telling him to go and wash himself as if that would wash it all away. Nick remembered looking at him and realizing that he'd just given up a friend and without ever really knowing that he'd considered André to be one. It was this that had shocked him and had enraged him. He'd thought he was better than that, but he wasn't.

"Es tut mir leid - I'm sorry," he jumped at the small voice coming out of the gloom and looked up into Connie's teary eyes. He gave a small bitter laugh and gestured for her to sit next to him, taking her hand in his, his other hand reaching out to caress her face, his fingers tracing their way across her skin. She smiled uncertainly and then leant forward and kissed him openly on his mouth. She jerked backwards looking shyly at him. "Everything's a bit fucked up for me at the moment," she shrugged her shoulders and shook her head, "but I don't want to talk about it, please, I'm sorry."

But Nick wasn't. He knew he didn't want to hear her stories, to know what she knew, to see what she'd seen. And he knew that she didn't want to hear his. He looked at her again, soaking in her visage and said, "Don't worry about it, we're all fucked up."

BERNIE'S BOMB

He'd been here for three days now and was just settling in, the sheets, at first strange, crisp, and cold, already softened to his contours. His hands clutched the edge of one and pulled it up over his head, a massive eyelid letting the white sunlight play in light orange figures across its surface. In the warmth of this cotton womb his childish smile, with teeth protruding slightly from between his lips, froze to an uncomfortable, smarting grimace as he remembered the woman from last week. That twisted, gnarled, fucking crazy old woman from last week. He ground his teeth angrily, - last week, last week, that was last fucking week, it was a shitty job sometimes - squeezed his eyes tightly shut, and tried divert himself with a quick assessment of Nick's flat-mate.

They'd been to a club, well, more of a red coloured slot in the wall called "Sorgen Brecher," a name he'd only taken note of because it literally meant care breaker, and that's what he needed at the moment. They'd inhaled the smoke of a hundred cigarettes, and who knows what else, because there was no ventilation to speak of. And they'd played more pinball than he'd ever played in his life because that's what was there - a bar and a pinball machine which they'd monopolised. He got the high score. And all the while they'd listened to a Spanish Samba all night long because that's what was on the tape deck.

He tried concentrating on the flatmate. What was he like? German, he was definitely German. What's that supposed to mean, he's German, says fuck

Apricot Juice and Other Stories...

all about him. He had jiggled to the Samba all night long. Except that he couldn't. It had been more like a nervous twitch in his buttocks. Halil started to giggle under the sheets and then pulled his face straight. Twitching buttocks were not necessarily an indication of mental instability, but belonged to a whole range of tell-tale characteristics. Intrusive behaviour, barely suppressed aggression, an insidious neurotic suspicion almost bordering on paranoia. Peter, pronounced Peh-ter as he had firmly pointed out, more than once, had problems, mainly with himself. He was, to all intents and purposes, fucked in the head.

Specifics? There had been a problem over money. Nick, who was lying next to Halil, snoring like a metal rasp on an iron railing, had told him about their argument. No, it wasn't money, it was the jokes about Peter and his money. That was it. He didn't like jokes on the subject of money, and Nick had made a joke about him paying the bill. He'd taken Nick ominously to one side and started shouting in his ear about not making jokes about money, he didn't like that, couldn't stand that. Shouted like he was losing control. Remembering him shouting, shaking, in front of Nick, bearing down upon Nick, took Halil straight back to the closed ward. To the dead, glaring eyes framed by the scraggy sweat of threadbare brown hair and the bizarre imitation of a smile, the mouth filled with stumps of teeth, flecked yellow and black. A witch. A bitch. A stupid fucking bitchwitch. He shuddered trying to think of Germany and Germans. War films, jackboots and Sieg

Heil's. The promised land for Bradford and London's skins. Arseholes. The fucking lot of them. Arseholes.

With this thought in mind he swept back the body warm sheets and duvet, springing out of bed shouting, "Deutschlander, Deutschlander raus, raus!" from the few words he knew, mainly gathered from the films he had seen. In the process he woke his spluttering friend, his crazy flatmate and probably the neighbours too. Holiday was holiday, after all.

Amid sleep sodden eyes he roared "Where's my bloody breakfast? C'mon you krauts and would be Huns, up and at 'em, get the kettle on, crack those eggs, don't burn those beans," pretending to be a mad Sergeant Major in a Butlins holiday camp.

Nick peered over at him trying to blink away the rawness of his hangover. "Halil, shut the fuck up and make your own fucking breakfast," he mumbled dourly. "And make us a coffee while you're at it." He rolled over and reached down to where his glasses were lying and let the world come into a grey, painful focus. The red pulsating diodes of his once modern radio alarm showed him that it wasn't time to get up, that he hadn't had enough sleep and that Halil was probably in need of a lobotomy. Halil wasn't what you called a good Muslim but he didn't drink 'white man's piss' as he affectionately called it, and didn't know or appreciate the body shagging, head splitting side affects of alcohol. It was one o'clock in the afternoon and almost ten hours before it was worth going out again. "And skin up!" he shouted, because the day was wasted whatever. Nick sunk his head back against the wall and shut his eyes in resignation.

He shook his head as drops of lizard cold water rolled across his cheek, tracing a clammy line slowly around the back of his neck. He yelled out loud at his reawakening. Halil chortled, offering him a tray with a cup of coffee, a roll smeared with cheese spread, a lighter, and a joint rolled as neatly and as tightly as your average commercial cigarette. Nick smiled as he took a sip of the hot, sweet, black coffee and reached for the spliff and the lighter. He muttered a friendly obscenity at Halil, and, with a wisping breath, sucked deeply on the joint.

He leant his head back on the wall, passing the joint limply to Halil who took it from him with two outstretched fingers and likewise took a drag. Nick hadn't seen Halil in almost a year, the last time he was in London. It was refreshing, having his old friend at his side spliffing and joking as the bright afternoon sun outside made his little room look dark on the inside. The pain slowly left his head as the warm blanket of hash gently settled across his body. He turned to face the face peeping cautiously around the door jamb, the sunlight glancing of a wide pair of metal rimmed pilot type glasses.

The face said "morgen," in an artificially contrived, coy, effeminate whimper. It was, of course, Klaus, Nick's flatmate, his short, sand coloured hair mussed sleepily into a coquettish quiff, his pale grey eyes flicking nervously from Nick to Halil and back.

The chilled out atmosphere became cold, Halil looking up at Klaus from the floor, his black brown eyes steel panned, ready for the anticipated rebuke. But Klaus was just trying to be friendly and wasn't too sure how. He eyed the two friends as if looking for a way into a locked room, but no-one was opening any doors. Then Nick offered him the joint, but he shook his head, tapping it with two fingers, and said, "Scheiß Briten, ihr seid verrückt " which literally translates as "Shitty British, you're all crazy," and is approximately what the two of them thought of him at that moment in time. He laughed his nervous laugh and closed the door.

Halil turned toward Nick. "What he say?" It was beginning to irritate that all around him indulged in that secret nasal babble, full of forceful V's and guttural CH's, which he was utterly unable to decipher. Under the influence he was prone to a little paranoia. Normally it was well roped in, but surrounded by this multitude of unknown words issued from unknown mouths, the ropes were beginning to fray. And Nick's room was so small, whitewashed and rectangular, with a bed, a desk and some books for decoration, the walls cool, almost clammy, cell like. He remembered how she'd glared at him as he sat there, eyeing him up and down as she sidled this way and that with her crabbed walk and crabbed gestures. He had pretended to read the paper, the glossed cold of the hospital wall icing his back as he watched her from the side of his eye, slowly shuffling in his direction, the frame of his glasses cutting a dim black line through the bleary scene. His buttocks squirmed on the hard bench as he edged a few more inches away from her.

Halil almost jumped as Nick answered, "Nothing. Just said we were crazy. You OK? Fuck him, ignore him. He's alright, just a bit weird. Gets a bit much at times, though." He sighed heavily. This was an understatement. He fell back onto the bed with a thud, and stared up at the ceiling. - Ah forget it - he thought, - it's not worth it, Halil's here, it's time to party, not to pine. - He rolled over to stub the butt of the joint out, looking over at Halil who rolled his eyes up at him.

"C'mon, let's get out of here," said Halil, exasperation bringing a tinging whine to his voice. "I got to get my bones in motion. Shit, we shouldn't have had that joint, you know. What's the plan?" he rubbed hard at his eyes, and squinted back at Nick.

There was a brief silence as Nick paused for consideration, which slowly filled with the dimmed shouts of playing children, the honk of a car horn, the stuttering song of a twittering bird. Nick's hoarse cough rattled through the small room as he tried to gather the warm mash of his thoughts together. "Grab a shower, then let's take a walk. It's walking weather. Then we're going to meet Clemens tonight, go for something to eat, have a drink. That's it I guess. You having a bad time here? We could shoot some pool." There was something of the plaintiff in his voice, a small and nagging fear that his friendship was going to the dogs, was drying up in the mound of distances, other priorities, girlfriends, houses, careers. Playing pool was a nostalgic thing, a college game he hardly ever played now. He'd moved away from London long ago, years, and still couldn't suss whether it was the right thing. He was away from his old mates, mixing with mad Germans, leading the disjointed life so common in Hamburg. A job here, a drink there, he needed a break, except that it all seemed like a holiday. He smiled fondly at Halil. Fuck it, he was here, that was all there was to it, and it wasn't all bad. Halil looked inquisitively back at him, the light glancing off his glasses so Nick could see a smear of grease where they'd been handled.

"What the fuck you looking at me like that for? Don't tell me that your latent homosexual tendencies have finally come to fruition in fucking nancy Nazi land." He grinned his toothy grimace of a grin and slowly stood up, the bed swaying slightly on its strange legs as he used its edge for support. He waved a long brown finger at it, saying, "Are you sure this bed was meant to be slept on, is this really what you call a safe construction?" The bed had been a peace offering to Nick from his flatmate after a particularly bad row. It consisted of a rickety wooden lattice made from a torn down fence. This was then balanced upon four thick feet of brown clay water pipes. These were corner pieces which curved around to give the impression that the bed was standing upon four terra cotta periscopes. Safe to say that this contraption was anything but safe, for if you leant upon any of its extremities the opposite side would slowly lift its tail in the air whilst the occupants hurriedly scrambled to the middle to restore balance and order. And Nick had been perfectly happy with his mattress and the floor. But, he had to admit, it did have a certain chaotic style to it, which was one of Klaus's redeeming characteristics.

Nick shook his head, laughing, but declining to answer. "Go and have a shower. There's a clean towel in the cupboard. Then let's get a bit of sun in. There's a great park near here. You stoned?"

"Nah, I'll be alright after the shower." He scratched at his crotch as he disappeared through the bedroom door. Nick sat back and closed his eyes once more.

Two showers and two hours later they were wandering slowly through the 'Planten un Blomen' garden park. The sound of crunched gravel and running water whispered along the sun dappled, wooded pathway. There was a slope and a curve in the path until it opened onto a wide, manmade platform, protruding out into the river and bordered with carved oak benches. The two took a seat on one of the benches and watched as a pair of black tailed swallows darted playfully across the water, the green and yellow fronds of the overhead willow framing the film-bred scene. Halil looked out across the bank in appreciation of German garden architecture.

"Fucking paradise this. You got a fag?" Nick, lying on his back staring into the white back-lit blue sky, his eyes smarting from the brightness and his throat dry from the dope, fumbled awkwardly in his jacket pocket. He brought out the cool gold packet and flicked at the bottom twice so that the cigarettes arranged themselves like the pipes of a church organ and pointed them vaguely in Halil's direction. After Halil had taken one he took another and stuck it into the corner of his parched mouth and waited for a light. After lighting his own cigarette Halil got up, walked round to Nick's head and sat down next to it, playing the flame of the lighter on the end of the cigarette. Nick felt his lungs asthmatically wheezing as he sucked in the smoke, but it didn't stop him.

Never did, never would, thought Halil to himself as Nick coughed like an old man and spat a yellowing globule of spit to the ground. "Why don't you give it up? Or you going to cough your guts up all day?"

Nick looked up at him through teary eyes, "Fuck you, fanny face. I can't give up 'till I got back all the fags you've cadged off me." With a sizzle and a sarcastic smile he threw the glowing end into the river. "You happy now?"

Halil pulled a face, "Aw man, don't go all sulky on me now, this is my fucking holiday." He looked around, nodding his head as if in agreement with himself. "This is a good place. Hamburg's good. It's good being here. Sometimes work is bad, know what I mean?" He leant back on his outstretched arm, as if he was staring dreamily into the sky, but what was going through his head was more of his very own nightmare.

He shuddered involuntarily. Through the glaze of the river water he saw her flattened runny nose, a silver moustache smeared across her upper lip as her dead eyed glare made his stomach turn. She'd been caught in the showers giving a blow job to that bastard Mason. He was what you called a bad man, a multiple rapist. They'd been fairly certain that he'd forced her to do it, but she said it was her choice so they couldn't put him in isolation. Halil wondered if Mason would've done it if he'd known what she was in for. She'd tried to castrate a man with a pair of scissors. A blunt pair of scissors according to the gossip.

She had nothing in her hands when she launched herself at Halil. But her bare hands were enough to put a stomach churning fear of God into him as he ran out of the ward, slamming the security door behind him, watching her clawing at the glass partition as if her hands were rats which could gnaw their way through. He wasn't squeamish, not normally, but it had got to him. Involuntary imaging, nightmares and shit. He'd needed the holiday. He blanked out the thought that he might need help.

Sunshine, and the nasal chatter of German, filtered into his dark reverie. He saw a small group of people coming around the bend, talking, a woman laughing too loudly, the bright colours of their clean, pressed clothes too loud. Halil sucked angrily on his cigarette, letting the smoke stream out of his nostrils, feeling it burn. He flicked it away with one hand and shook the dozing Nick with the other. "C'mon, lets walk." And stood up.

Halil felt dirty as they loped through the yellow

and blue manicured flower beds of the park, past the white washed walls of the herbal garden. He knew there was no need. But he always felt slightly soiled, as if he'd washed in muddy waters, when he was walking amongst the stiff, crisp clothes of the middle class. All cord and canvas, safe and styleless. "This is a fucking white man's land here. Look at them all, all fucking scrubbed and polished marble white. You see a black man here? You see a Paki? Show us one. Go on."

Nick sighed audibly, stopping and rubbing at his eyes, the fingers of both hands behind his glasses like a horde of pink windscreen wipers. Halil looked at him. He looked like a squirrel when he did that. He always had. Nick squinted back, tired affection smiling in his reddened eyes. "You fucking brown nosed Paki, you got a problem you have. What's that there - black as spades he is." He nodded at a black guy sauntering down the walkway.

Halil ground his teeth and screwed up his face in mock anger, and started shouting loudly, "I'll tell what he is, he's unhappy he is, fucking unhappy. And you know why? No, 'course you don't. Of course you don't, 'cos you're one of THEM paleface middle class whitey boys. You are, you fucking are. He's unhappy 'cos he's lonely, fucking lonely he is. I bet he's the only black man in a five mile radius. I bet he's as lonely as a fucking trout in a swarm of fucking piranhas." He was enjoying himself now. He watched satisfied as Nick doubled over, his body creased in two, with his hee-hawing, see-sawing laughter.

Apricot Juice and Other Stories...

Nick straightened up, a sleepy tear dribbling out of the corner of his eye. He ran his hand through his hair and shook his head. "Nutter, a fucking nutter," he muttered. He looked around towards the octagonal café nearby, with its black stained wooden lattice providing a chequered sun shelter. "C'mon let's grab a coffee," he said wiping at the tear which had rolled down his cheek.

They sat themselves down at the rickety folding tables, their cups and their elbows resting on the flaking wooden slats. Halil started scratching at the remains of the varnish with a key he'd produced from his pocket. Nick watched him, his chin resting on his fisted hands. He could've been bored, but his expression gave nothing away. He sipped languidly at his black coffee. "What's up with you? Something's bugging you."

In reply Halil stuck his little finger into his left nostril and twisted it carefully to the left and then to the right. Extracting it, he peered closely at the thick strand of phlegm clinging to the tip of his finger. He rolled it carefully between his thumb and little finger until it formed a grey brown bogey. He flicked it casually away with his forefinger, watching it land unseen on the violet overcoat belonging to an old white haired woman. He stared down into his coffee, avoiding any possible eye contact. He looked sideways at Nick. "Nothing's wrong. I just needed a break. I'm having a break. So everything's fine, alright? And yourself?" He was slightly irritated. He'd forgotten how intrusive his friend could be. He'd worked too much. He'd forgotten his friend. He shook his head as if he were guilty of something and could shake it off. "It's not that really, it's just this fucking life. Don't get me wrong, I like my job. It's like you gain respect, people come to me for advise nowadays. Y'know, people who when I started I thought they knew everything, and now they come to me." He chewed at a fingernail, looked at it carefully, chewed again.

Nick nodded, "That's good, isn't it? I get fuck all respect at my job. You know what they ask me there? They ask me whether I cleaned the fucking bogs properly."

Halil laughed, and then looked at Nick, his nose rodently twitching, "What you doing here anyway? Cleaning fucking lavatories. With your qualifications you could get yourself a proper job. You got qualifications coming out your arse. Go'n' work for a change. Cleaning lavatories. You can wash my arse if you need to do something dirty that bad."

Nick looked hurt and started to whine, "It is proper work, and I need the free time. You tell me a job that pulls in three hundred a week for ten hours work. You got one I'll take it, but up to now there's been no offers."

Halil ignored him, holding his fingernails up to the light as he went on, "But the job gets to you sometimes. It has to. The people I deal with are fucking disturbed. Not sort of borderline cases, but no longer socially functioning animals. It doesn't matter how much society changes, these people are not going to be a part of it." Halil stared up behind Nick's head as her

Apricot Juice and Other Stories...

image flooded back, clawing its way toward him. He forced it out of his mind and tried to concentrate on Nick.

Nick felt irritated at Halil's broad statement. Not only was it wrong, Halil was avoiding the issue. Agitated, he flicked the table top with his fingernails. "That's not the point though, this is about you, not them. What's going on in you?" Nick yawned and rubbed at his nose, all the while keeping Halil in his visage.

Halil stretched in accordance with Nick's yawn, and said, "That's what I mean though, look, the job might have it's disturbing moments, it's not surprising if you're working with a bunch of nutters. But that's not it. I like the job, it's what I guess you'd call fulfilling. And it's not like these people start making you ask are you crazy or not, it's the opposite. They make you feel sane. But the whole thing makes you ask what's the sense in it. Know what I mean? Like when we were at college, we wanted to go places. We had dreams. I wanted to be creative, not just another fucking social worker. I know I've done loads of things and been places I never thought possible, but it's like here's thirty, and here's your life and thank you very much. There's got to be more, hasn't there?"

He took sip of his coffee and looked back at Nick. "I feel stale sometimes, and there's got to be more to life than feeling stale." But Halil didn't feel stale, he felt frightened. So frightened that he couldn't tell his friend about the sleep crushing nightmares, about the glimpses of madness crawling at the edges of his waking hours. Better to regurgitate old conversations than bring that up. He shivered as he felt the hiss of her breath on his neck, wiped his hand across his clammy brow and stared hard at Nick. He felt as if he was betraying their friendship, but he couldn't tell him.

Nick, oblivious to the source of Halil's discomfort, let out a rush of air in a loud sighing breath. "Why? Why has there got to be more to life than feeling stale? 'Specially if you don't take the risks. Look, you're a home base man, and you like it that way. You got a good career, a house, a girlfriend you love, it's what you opted for. If you want something else then you got to take the risk." Nick, as was often the case, remained unconvinced by his own words.

But Halil wasn't listening, he'd heard it all before. And it pissed him off. Everything was the wrong way around. Nick shouldn't be cleaning toilets. Halil punched him sharply on the arm. "Get a fucking proper job you lazy arse."

Nick rubbed his arm and ignored the challenge. He rested his head on his arms, folded before him on the flimsy table, his eyes following the rolling walk of a young woman coming towards them. She caught his look and smiled in return, but his mouth merely twitched, his face generally being in no kind of mood to start smiling at people. He swivelled his head round as he watched her sway away until he jumped as Halil thumped him again. "Stop fucking ogling, you horrible little man. You'll get us arrested."

"Stop fucking hitting me," whined Nick, leaning back in his seat, rubbing at his aching arm. They were both tired, and getting bored. "We could grab some kip if you want."

"Naw man, I'm fine. Let's walk someplace. When we meeting Clemens?" His hand brushed quickly at a frond of his black hair which had worked itself loose from his pony tail and fallen across his face.

Nick swirled the remains of his coffee round in the cup and downed them with an exaggerated slurp. He stood to his feet, using the arms of his chair to lever himself upwards as if he were a fat, old mafiosi. His face cracked open in a wide mouthed yawn, and he needed to lean on Halil's shoulder to support it. "I dunno, 'bout ten, what time you got?"

Halil rolled back his coat sleeve and peered at his watch. "It's ten to seven already. What the fuck've we done all day?"

"Nothing, what else? My stomach's a fucking rumbling, let's go eat something. There's a nice 'talian place on the corner from here." He yawned again, staggering with the effort. He shook his head and smiled weakly at Halil. "Hope I make it to tonight."

"'Course you will, 'course you will. You'll be fine after we eat." He paused, looking around, a little disoriented. "Uhh, which way is it?"

Nick grabbed him by the arm, guiding him along towards the path, "C'mon, this way, this way." They walked, Nick dragging slightly behind, chattering a bit over his shoulder about a suit he was going to buy, about the new woman in his office, about how good looking the women in Hamburg were, about nothing in particular. Nick said nothing, as was his wont when Halil was on a chatting roll. So they lolled along, slowly, lazy, happy. And then Halil stopped short, peering up into the sky.

"What the fuck is that!" he shouted at Nick, his arm raised, pointing into the air.

Nick looked at him blankly, and then looked up to the skyline. "Oh that. That's the television tower. I thought I showed it you."

"You showed me fuck all since we been here, apart from some smoky bars and strange smelling Germans. That is amazing. It's like something out of fucking Star Trek. Like beam me up Scotty." Careering out of the ground before them, neck breakingly straight up into the air, was a smooth white rounded column which, some hundred feet up, skewered a saucer shaped disk, which hangs in the Hamburg skyline like a clichéd visitor from outer space.

Nick laughed at Halil's amazement, no longer impressed having lived in the shadow of this gargantuan for the last years. "We can go up there if you want, you can see most of Hamburg from up there. Costs though."

"Ah, fuck that, let's go eat, I'm starving. And I can't stand sightseeing." So they walked on past the winding footbridge which traverses the wide birth of the Karolinen Straße. The bridge runs directly into the mouth of the tower as if it were a feedway rather than a footpath, delivering countless hapless humans to their fate in the pristine monstrosity. A mix of modern futurism and ancient spectacle.

But Nick and Halil were not interested in the building. Nick and Halil were interested in the rumbling implosion in their stomachs and the bitter acid taste in their mouths. They were hungry. So they walked on past the old, brown stoned, ex-Jewish school without looking up, and crossed a gently cobbled side street without looking into the Italian alleyway, quaintly filled with hanging gardens and recessed balconies.

They walked on until they reached the corner of the Marktstraße where the Italian restaurant was nestled. Its patio looks out onto both streets and was filled with munching guests packed around white Formica tables, sitting on green, slatted, fold-away chairs. But Nick didn't stop to see if there was a free seat to be squeezed into, he marched Halil into the restaurant and took the table set into a recess between two whitewashed pillars. The whole place was white-washed, the walls lined with a roughly swirled plaster finish which bit into your back if you leant against it. Various plants and bushes poked their leaves between the pillars, searching for sunlight in the dimly lit room. Nick motioned to Halil to sit and muttered at him "The tuna fish pizza only costs six marks, 'bout two quid, and tastes too."

"Sounds good to me. Let's hit it." He sat back in his chair, ran both his hands through his hair, and clasped them at the back of his head, his brown eyes running up and down the approaching waitress.

Seeing his look Nick turned round to peer likewise. He jumped as Halil deftly clipped him across the top of his turned head. He looked angrily at Halil. "Will you stop fucking hitting me, it's getting on my tits," he almost snarled.

"Sorry, sorry. My, my, we're bloody nervy today aren't we?" He grabbed at the flour speckled Italian bread the girl had brought in a brown plastic woven bread basket, smeared it roughly with the hot, runny garlic butter, and stuffed it whole into his mouth. All the while he watched expressionless as Nick ordered them a bottle of mineral water, a beer, two minestrone soups and two tuna fish pizzas. Halil felt the saliva gush into his mouth as he pictured the food on his plate.

They both ate quickly and noisily, slurping their soups, gobbling the pizzas, guzzling their drinks and smacking their lips. Halil belched loudly, Nick glanced at him over his glasses, a wry smile across his face. They didn't exchange a word until they'd both finished. "That was goood," purred Halil. Nick nodded in agreement, pursing his lips in appreciation, and then dragging a white napkin across them, leaving it lying crumpled up on his empty plate. And then he belched too. Surprised, Halil coughed in Nick's direction, his brow furrowed lightly in disapproval. "You used to have the best table manners I ever saw," he said accusingly, tapping his fork absentmindedly on the edge of the table as if to reinforce his words.

Nick smiled, pleased by the compliment, amused by Halil's evident lack of grasp of the passing of time. "That was over ten years ago. And if anyone taught me to eat like a barbarian then it was you. I am now in the dubious position of being able to eat harmoniously in all forms of company, whether they be kings and queens or lowly black faced coal workers. 'Sides, eating is all the more pleasurable when you can hear what you're doing." He belched again.

"What you trying to say, that you're now a bonafide member of the working class just 'cos you've forgotten how to eat properly? Takes a lot more than that, my son." His finger was wagging preposterously, admonishingly in the air. "What you're missing is the aspiration to be middle class. Every fucker I know from back home wants a nice house, with a long garden at the back, and double garage with a Ford for her and a Jaguar for him, and the fucking manners to match. With those manners all you can mix with is other middle class mummy's boys who want to act like they got a past." And with that he rolled a bread crumb in his finger and flicked it at Nick's forehead. Then he looked at his watch. "It's half eight," he said, his voice tinged with impatience, his words elongated as he stressed them.

Nick put his hand under his shirt and scratched at his shoulder. "And? You going someplace?" As the waitress came by he caught her eye and ordered another beer for himself and an orange juice for Halil. "Try and relax. For me. We're not in a rush here, look around, no-one is. You noticed how slow everyone walks 'round here. They've got time. If you ask me this job's doing your head in."

Halil started as if Nick had removed the top of his head and taken a peek inside. "What should I do?" he asked nervously. But it had been an off-the-cuff remark which Nick forgot as soon as it had been said. The door to the restaurant creaked loudly beside them as it swung open.

Nick turned round to look at the restaurant's new arrivals, a couple both dressed in tight fitting black terylene casual suits, he with a bright orange shirt, and collar length wavy hair, dyed a ferocious blue black, while she had on a translucent purple shirt with extra long lapels, and close cropped, yellow bleached hair. They were both tanned to a ridiculous Barby doll brown. Nick swallowed theatrically and moved his gaze back to Halil. He looked him up and down, smiled vacantly and answered, "Dunno. You tried Prozac?"

Halil gaped at him wide eyed and open mouth-ed, and then laughed. "You fucking little git. Not bad, not bad. Actually I have tried it. Once, but it doesn't do a thing. It doesn't give you a buzz, 'cos it works on blood concentration. So you have to let it build up over a week or two before it starts really working, but the change is so gradual that you don't notice it happening. So I didn't get a thing from it. Valium's better. That knocks you right out."

Halil coughed loudly and picked at his nose, then leant forward. "Tell me something. What happened to your mate Al?"

"Al? That at the airport, you mean? His old man sorted that out. Kicked up a real stink. Pulled in some favours. They actually managed to get the Germans to arrest the two arseholes who beat up Al. I don't think they were done for anything, but Al was let free after that. It was fucking hairy at the time though. Don't think he'll be coming back here, either."

Halil raised his eyebrows and shook his head in disbelief. He looked at his watch again, and fidgeted in his chair, sliding his buttocks this way and that. He stared down at his plate, empty except for a few smears of fat and a couple of obstinate crumbs of food. He flicked one with his finger but kept staring at the white circle, his gaze being drawn to its cold, white gloss. He felt his chest constricting, the panic clutching and rising, fine droplets of sweat eking out onto his forehead. He looked at the plate and it began to darken, it began to glower back at him, an eye, a black, white-rimmed eye, her eye. He gritted his teeth and swallowed hard, clenching white- knuckled at the rim of the table. "Get a grip, get a fucking grip," he hissed to himself, and then he had it, the eye receded, his breathing deepened, and, with a full cheeked sigh, he let out the air clenched in his lungs. "When're we going?" he asked after a short silence.

A scratch of his nose and Nick, oblivious to everything, answered, not without irritation in his voice, "How about after we pay. In a minute. I'll just give Clemens a call, see if he's at home."

As Nick rose to leave the table Halil grabbed at his shirt sleeve, stopping him short. "Is it far? I don't want to be traipsing all over the place." His voice lilted with its whine.

"Hey, it's just 'round the corner, keep yer fucking hat on. And stop moaning, it'll be good to-night." He flicked his arm free, turning sharply away, his head ducking quickly under the overhanging branch of an overgrown pot plant. Nick always felt like a boxer when he ducked like that, bobbing his head quickly down and to one side. And like a fraud, because he'd never had a proper boxing match in his life, just short flurries of fists and feet, sometimes painful, sometimes not, and the last one of those was fifteen years ago. But he still liked the thought of weaving and dodging, and the various trees and bushes he'd come up against hadn't caught him yet.

So he gave a boxer's nod to the waiter behind the steel topped bar and asked for the 'phone. The waiter gave him a cheesed-off waiter's glare and told him that the 'phone was in the passageway leading to the toilets. Nick took the opportunity to relieve himself before contacting Clemens. A quick word with the man to see if it was alright to go up and he returned to Halil. There was a jaunty spring in his step, now that they had a concrete rendezvous to distract them from talking about their somewhat embarrassing lives. He smiled openly at Halil, sat down, and looked over his shoulder trying to catch the dour waiter's eye so they could pay and be off.

Apricot Juice and Other Stories...

"How much is it?" asked Halil, spilling a handful of crumpled notes and coins of mixed denomination onto the table. "Go on. Take it, I don't get this funny money."

Nick carefully extracted a fifty mark note and handed it to the waiting waiter, adding on a couple of marks tip. The waiter, his dickey bow slightly askew, pressed a five mark coin into Nick's hand as change. Nick thanked him cordially and then made a face at Halil. "Grab your jacket and let's get out of here."

Nick strode purposefully out of the restaurant, Halil lagging behind, tugging his jacket sleeve up his outstretched arm, walking sideways out of the door, almost tripping over his half running feet. He grunted at Nick, but Nick wouldn't wait for him and just walked on round the corner. Halil broke into a run and grabbed him by the shoulder.

"What the fuck's up with you? Slow down. What's up?" he asked, infuriated by Nick's strange behaviour.

"We're up by twenty marks. He forgot to charge us for the drinks. I wanted to get out before he noticed. C'mon, it's just round the corner." He was panting lightly with excitement, his eyes darting from side to side as if he were a suspicious character in an old "B" movie.

He put his hand on Halil's elbow, urging him along, but Halil shook his arm free, tutting like a disparaging old woman and shaking his head slowly. "Hey, you used to be so honest you wouldn't take the last sweet in a packet, 'case someone else wanted it."

"Times change, and I'm not exactly rich or anything. 'Sides, I still don't take the last biscuit if I can help it. That's just manners, that is." Nick's voice was loud and smiling, he was almost falling over with childish pride at Halil's consternation. Giggling, he tried to needle Halil. "What's up with you, you secretly joined the flying squad, or MFI, or what?"

Halil smiled, but scrutinized his friend as they walked along. He noted the ash grey flecking the short cropped, dark brown hair, the tiny rivulets of folded patterns of skin, tugging at the corner of his eye, the thickening of his face which made his eyes look even smaller. His thickening midriff. His skin still had its unblemished prepubescent shine and the look in his eye was angrily alive, but he was showing the signs of age, the signs of change. Halil rubbed the back of his neck, and looked away, down at the shit strewn pavement. He felt defused, bemused, as if the world were losing its contours.

They had reached the corner into the Glashütten Straße. The gaudy colours of the flower shop and the swirled motifs of the hairdresser's appeared vaguely familiar to Halil. "Hey, have I been here before?" he asked.

"Sure. Last time you were here. I used to live here, remember. Clemens lived opposite. You remember?" Halil remembered and nodded. What he remembered though was a different colour, a flaking, serious grey, not the bright blues and reds which faced them as they stood before the steep steps leading up to the main door. The acrid smell of sprayed urine which pushed back Halil's nose was still the same. He wrinkled it in disgust as Nick reached up to press the top of the row of black bell-buttons. He waited until they heard the electric burr of the door lock and leant heavily on the thick panelled door, jerking his shoulder as the lock caught momentarily in its catch. The door popped open and Nick fell in, Halil following on his heels.

Together they took a deep breath as they stood at the bottom of the stairwell, gaping skyward. The stairs curved steeply up toward the roof of the house, metal supporting struts crisscrossing the lurching space between, making the whole structure an ungainly, rickety affair. Halil grabbed the single banister and shook it firmly. It's metal rungs rattled loosely in answer. "You sure this is safe?"

Just then a voice came floating down from above, "Nick, Halil? Come up!" They both turned their heads skywards, but only Nick could see Clemens' head as he leaned over the bannister. Clemens waved theatrically, Nick waved back. "'Course it's safe," he said smiling at Halil, and started climbing the steps, "C'mon," he shouted back at Halil.

The landings of each floor were differently lit and individually lined with various paraphernalia. Halil looked in amazement at the fridge-freezer on the first floor, stumbled into an old coal oven in the dimness of the second floor, panting a little as he passed the brightly lit row of a dozen pair of shoes standing next to a greasy blue bin on the third, stumbling to a wheezing stop as he reached the fourth floor, and saw Clemens grinning face. He hung onto the bannister and looked around, the landing packed with wooden boxes, an old washing machine, and, on top of this, a baby's bath filled with earth and planted with what looked like a small tree, and a willowing ratchet of green ferns. Vertically strung in the well between the landing and stairs was a punch ball. Coughing, he felt his hand been taken by Clemens and being pumped up and down. His deep bass boomed out with a thick German accent, "Hallo Halil and how are you doing today?" Halil could only look, smile, and nod his head, trying to catch his breath. "You are a little unfit maybe? Never mind, come in. We smoke a joint now." And Clemens shot a loud laugh across the landing, patting Halil on the back while directing him into the living room of his flat. He turned to Nick, "What have you done with your friend, he is almost dying I think?"

Nick, who had almost recovered, spluttered, "fucking stairs, when're you going to get a lift? How you keeping Clemens?" He gave the big man a hug, a little cumbersome since he only just topped five foot five, whereas Clemens towered above him at well over six foot and was not what you called thin.

Halil and Nick sank into the massive, deep blue, corduroy sofas. They were old early eighties seating arrangements, made up of big blocks of foam filled material, which you could manoeuvre to your taste, or fall between when drunk or stoned. Almost by

Apricot Juice and Other Stories...

accident they toned into the grey blue carpet, which in turn set in contrast a massive, ornate picture frame, containing nothing but a deep red velvet surface. Hanging on the adjacent wall were four paintings of a woman's eye, almost identical except for the change of shades and colours as the viewer moved from eye to eye. Placed at strategic points in the room, within reach of the sofas, were four large ceramic elephants, encrusted with a glazed, bright blue, white, and yellow, erratically arranged mosaic. Their trunks held high, and backs flattened, they made useful little side tables. Halil eyed the professional stereo system enviously, and stroked the rounded metallic surface of the globed speaker, perched upon its stalk standing next to him. Lighting was provided by a single shaded overhead bulb beneath which hung an old disco reflecting sphere, off which the light happily sprung when it was set in spinning motion. Although it was not immediately obvious that two musicians lived here, no-one was surprised when they found out.

Clemens plumped himself down opposite the two and offered both a smile which was widened by the spread of his arms along the sofa-back behind him, and the long stretch of his legs out in front of him. "Are you hungry? Or do you want drinks? Something to drink?" he asked cordially. "A beer?"

Halil shook his head, "Uhh, I don't drink alcohol," he said, slightly embarrassed.

"Sorry, I forgot, you're a Mohammedan aren't you."

Halil started, "I'm a what?" he asked, puzzled. Then his face cleared as he realized what Clemens meant. "Oh right. A Muslim, yeah, I'm a Muslim. No alcohol. I'm Alcohol-frei." He laughed at his joke and looked over to Nick.

Clemens went on. "Yes, a Mohammedan, that's right. No problem, no problem, I have alcohol-freies beer if you want. Or water, or tea. A nice cup of tea for the Englishman?" He looked at Nick, who started to giggle.

"Orange juice is fine. You already been smoking?" he asked, and then gestured at the music centre, "mind if I have a look at this, that's a DAT player isn't it?"

Clemens nodded his slightly thinning head of close cropped, fine, light brown hair "Yes it is, and I have smoked only a little bit." He fumbled around in his pocket, extracting a crumpled piece of cigarette paper. "You want to make a joint? I get the drinks, you make the joint, I play some music soon." He handed the piece of paper to Halil, who unravelled it to reveal a small chocolate brown slab of hash. Clemens walked out of the room after pointing to the lighter, the cigarette papers and the cigarettes lying on top of one of the elephants.

Halil reached over for the papers and extracted three of them. He gave one of them a long tongued lick and stuck it carefully to the back of one of the others so that the outer edges formed an incomplete V. He took the third paper and stuck it across the top of the wide end of this V and turned them over, the little fingers of both hands held outstretched during the whole process. He then took a cigarette and rolled its end between forefinger and thumb before the loosened tobacco began to trickle out of its end. He gently forced the tobacco out of the cigarette into a little mound on the waiting papers. He spread this out along the middle of the V, leaving a short space at its narrow end, and took the tablet of hash in one hand, the lighter in the end. Pinching the hash between the fingernails of thumb and forefinger he proceeded to heat the lump, sucking the emanating wisps of grey smoke in through his hovering nose, whisking the lighter away when the hash started to glow, wetting a finger and dabbing at it to put it out. He then crumbled it into the tobacco, his hands moving the length of the papers. He looked up as Clemens placed a glass of orange juice on the little table, nodding his head in thanks, but not saying a word. Clemens and Nick watched him intently going about his business. They too were silent. Halil took the packet of cigarettes and ripped a small square of card from the inside of the box lid. He rolled this into a little tube and placed it in the space at the narrow end of the papers. He took the lot in both hands and proceed to roll it back and forth through his fingers. At all times his little fingers had remained outstretched as if he were an English grandmother drinking her afternoon tea. He licked along the edge of the paper and deftly stuck it down with a single run through his fingers. He tapped the joint once on the table and then twisted its open end closed. He bit this end off and spat it out into the ashtray, ceremoniously, but holding the joint up in the air for inspection with a critical air.

He politely passed it over to Clemens who held it to the light, turning it in his fingers, and nodded to Halil in appreciation. He put the reefer to his lips, took a match, wiped it across the box, and put the flame to the end of the joint, and inhaled deeply. He held his breath for a few seconds and then exhaled with a loud sigh, and then began to cough wretchedly. With a look of sorry consternation at his untimely outburst pulling at the corner of his eyes he passed the joint back to Halil and reached for the bottle of water he had brought in from the kitchen. He gulped at it thirstily, burping loudly as he placed it back on the table, shaking his head. "It isn't weak, is it?" he asserted, laughing at the incapacity of his lungs. "And I am not so young as before."

Halil smiled indulgently at him as Nick reached out for the joint. Halil took another quick toke before handing it over with a sputtered, "Here, take it." He looked back at Clemens, saying, "Clemens, what about the women you promised us? I seem to remember you being a pop star and all that, so what about the group-ies?"

Clemens smiled and shook his head again. "Halil, that was many years ago. Now I am old and fat with no hair, and not a pop star but a Künstler, an artist."

Nick chimed in, "Does this mean that all the

women you know now are old and fat and losing their hair?" He laughed at his own inanity.

Clemens laughed too, but retorted, saying "No, it means that they are now all much too perverse for your English Geschmack."

"Perverse, perverse," shouted Halil slightly wildly, "nothing wrong with perverse. Tell Uncle Halil about perverse. How perverse?"

Clemens guffawed his belly wobbling laugh, bursting into a fit of coughing at the end. He clapped his chest with his fist and smiled again at Halil and Nick. "They like fat men with no hair. This is very perverse."

"Aw Clemens, if they saw me they'd forget about fat men with no hair, I can promise you that," Halil answered, his voice high with its sneer of sarcasm. "Fat fetishes are really no problem for me, I'm a mental health worker, I can sort them out in no time at all. Go on, give 'em a call." He jumped nervously as the telephone emitted its tinny bird whistle. Clemens leapt to his feet, sweeping the receiver into one hand, taking the telephone in the other. After hearing who was on the other end he winked at the two on the sofa and sidled out into the hallway.

Halil was once again startled at how quickly the big man moved. He remembered him from last time because he made the impression that he was the only non-neurotic German around. They'd all gone to his little studio, and messed around trying to make some music, smoking and generally just pissing around. It had been a good time, just hanging out, but most of all Halil remembered two things about Clemens. His deep resonating voice, and just how warm hearted and laid back he was. Halil had told him, "Clemens, you have got to be one of the coolest people I've ever met." Clemens had just laughed his gut quaking guffaw, patted Halil on the shoulder, and said, "Yes, I know how much difficulties you must all have with this, but you must not worry because I like you very much." Halil returned to the present as Clemens walked back into the room. He looked satisfied, as if he'd eaten a large meal.

"Bad news?" asked Nick. He took a drag on the remains of the joint, pulled a bitter face, and stubbed it emphatically out in the ashtray. The soft grey pillows of stonedom, spiced with the tiny razors of paranoia, were beginning to roll over him, and he felt a manic urge to jump up, to talk to some people, maybe to dance. "Let's go to the pub," he said, not waiting for Clemens to answer.

"C'mon, relax, let's just sit here a bit and talk," said Halil, who was starting to mellow out and wasn't particularly into pubs anyway, alcohol not being on his list of preferred recreational drugs.

But it was Clemens who decided. "We must go for a drink to celebrate," he said as he sat down and started pulling on his trainers over his blue stockinged feet. Without waiting for the obvious question he went on, "We must celebrate Halil's...what is Anwesenheit?...Anyway, we must celebrate Halil. And we must celebrate me, because we have dates for a tour now in Switzerland next month."

Despite the danger of the onset of an almighty lethargy Halil decided that he couldn't argue with this, and pulled himself up to grab his jacket. "Alright, I'm game. Let's hit it."

They all started to scramble out of their seats, rooting around the room for their jackets, their shoes, their balance. Then a quick check in the mirror, Halil ran a hand through his hair, Nick a comb, Clemens didn't bother looking and they were ready to go. "Where to?" asked Nick, then pointing to the elephant table, saying, "don't forget the drugs."

Clemens walked over and pocketed the little twist of paper, the cigarettes and the lighter. Halil noticed what he was wearing. A pair of loose hanging, wash greying chinos, a faded red sweatshirt, stretched at the collar, and a pair of cheap red basketball boots, the little rubber ankle disc on the left shoe half torn away. Halil felt smart in his serge Marines jacket, the well pressed whorls of his mauve paisley shirt, the comfortable fall of his dark blue Wrangler jeans and the buffed up black shine of his Paul Smith shoes. And he felt sorry for Clemens' obvious poverty, the stretched fade of his clothes. He was suddenly embarrassed for even thinking like this at all, the blood rushed hot to his face, his neck prickling with perspiration. He felt his heart hammering in his chest, his breath speeding up and shallowing out. He swallowed and tried to gather his thoughts but the dope drew them out in long inconsequent trails. He noticed the painful tug of his overfilled bladder just in time. "I got to go to the bathroom," he almost yelped, hurrying to the toilet, where he quickly relieved himself, one hand outstretched for support, leaning on the wall in front as if he was going to retch. Grinding his teeth hard together, he clumsily packed his cock back where it belonged, the red tails of his shirt trying to escape through his fly, swearing at the inevitable last drops of piss leaking out, washed his hands, and, removing his glasses, splashed the cold water into his face, rubbing at his eyes. He told himself to pull it together, these people were his friends, no panic now, no madness now, took a deep breathe and walked out into the hall to the others.

They filed out of the flat, onto the landing, wound down the stairs, tramping out into the street. The sun was just sinking behind the burning roof tops, but none of them paid any attention to the skyline. For them it was eyes straight ahead, don't look left, don't look right, march right on down to the "Markstube."

The "Markstube" is an establishment basically consisting of thick slabs of wood carved into the various items of furniture necessary to have a drink. Occasionally these are sanded down and repainted. The first thing the visitor sees on entering is the massively hewn bar, roughly twelve feet long, curving off at one end by the window, where a bench has been set into the wall. Opposite the bar are two fixed tables with simple cut backed benches which serve to form two waist high booths. These are painted in metallic green to match the bar, while the backs of the benches are painted orange. Customers can sit there, or perch at the bar on the wobbly stools, or go up a few steps to another booth, with a table running parallel to the wall, and a large cold window behind. At the back, another couple of steps higher, is a small games room which used to have some of the best table football in Hamburg, until the table was stolen. Now, instead of the clack and crack of surely struck balls, all that is heard is the electronic whine and whistles of two pinball machines. In the middle of this room is a tall, ovally cut table, bolted to the floor boards, and ringed by a couple more of those spindly stools.

The three crowded in at the bar in front of Mac and ordered two bottles of Jever for Nick and Clemens and an orange juice for Halil. Mac runs the bar, and has done for twenty years. An ex-sailor made good with a well situated pub for which he paid little rent. A typical sailor with a smidgen of several languages and close cropped white grey hair, the toil of his many years of whiskey consumption was beginning to make itself shown in the shape of his ever expanding belly. He was short and stout, and the perfect dog for him would have been a mastiff, both in terms of a dangerous temperament and the look of a barrel. Clemens exchanged a few pleasantries with him, and then motioned the other two to take one of the booths further down the pub.

The three slid along the benches of the booth until they were comfortably accommodated, Nick and Halil seated opposite Clemens, supping his beer and lighting a cigarette. All three had the aura of the dazed as they glanced around, searching for attractive faces among the dozen or so people populating the pub.

"Man, this stuff's strong," whined Nick, coughing throatily. "I'm fucking rubbered," he said, looking directly at Halil as if he had just said something of major import.

"Me too," agreed Halil, his tone complying with the significance of this piece of information. He momentarily leant against the wall, Clemens looked at him as if he were worried.

"What is rubbered?" a confused Clemens asked Nick. Both Nick and Halil put their heads together as they started to giggle.

"My nose is rubbered," tittered Nick.

"My arse is definitively rubbered," wheezed Halil, breaking into a raw, grunting, coughing laugh. He leant on the table, putting a hand on Nick's shoulder for support.

Clemens winced visibly, shaking his head at their obvious madness, but a little stung at this childish alienation. "What is this rubbered?" he bayed, loud more for effect than with emotion. The two bent their heads down, staring at the table surface like two secretly unrepentant schoolboys, having been beaten down by the admonishments of their Headmaster.

Nick ran his fingernail along the etched out grooves scarring the woodwork, took a deep breath and sat up to face Clemens. "Rubbered is what you feel like when you're stoned. Like my nose feels like rubber. His arse feels like rubber. We're rubbered," he explained in mock solemnity.

Clemens nodded. "Ah. I see." Then he reached over and pinched Nick's nose between his thumb and forefinger. Nick jerked his head back in surprise and Clemens barked out a laugh. "It's true. Your nose feels like rubber." Contemplatively he likewise pinched his own nose. "Ahh. My nose as well feels like rubber. This means I must be rubbered too. Or not?"

The question mark was thrown at Halil who was still slumped across the table, eyeing up his somewhat sticky orange juice. He unsuccessfully attempted to elevate himself to the height of the others, but settled for a raise of his eyebrows, his eyeballs rolling somewhere in Clemens' direction. "Clemens," he said as emphatically as he could, "you are most definitely rubbered. In fact you were probably rubbered before rubber was even invented, that's how rubbered you are. I would even go as far to say," he pause for dramatic effect, coughing a little to emphasise the contrast between the eternity of his wisdom and the mortality of its bearer, "that you have been rubberised."

Clemens looked worried, looked bored, and looked worried again. He supped at his beer, peered into the smoke filled air as if in meditation, gave Halil a mildly penetrating glance and asked, "this rubberised, I think it is good, yes?"

"Very good," answered the two friends in absolute unison. All three broke into sudden laughter, causing heads to turn, Clemens banging the table in appreciation of their little druggy performance.

Clemens waved his hand at Mac, signalling for another round of drinks. Mac nodded crustily, Clemens sighed, placing both hands flat on the table as if he were about to leave. He leant over to Nick. "Hey Nick, I have some good business for you," he said, the side of his mouth smiling like a Cockney ticket tout.

"What's that Clemens? What sort of business you got for me?" Nick conspiratorially scratched the side of his nose.

Clemens smiled, "Good business, very good business. You remember I owe you the fifteen marks?"

Nick nodded his head. "'Course I do, 'course I do, there's no reason why I should forget, is there?" he was already smirking, seeing Clemens' bright eyed laughing look. Sometimes he found it funny just hearing Clemens speaking English in his good humoured fashion, the words often twisted round back to front, flattened in the tilt of the accent.

"Yes, yes, no, I mean no, no, of course not. But this fifteen marks?"

Nick sighed, "Yeah, what about the fifteen marks?"

"You maybe like to make it twenty five?"

"Uhh, yeah, sure," answered Nick, a little confused.

Clemens roared with laughter as he held out his hand, "then please give me ten, then the fifteen is now twenty five."

Nick reached into his pocket, shaking his head as he laughed with Clemens. He placed a green twenty mark note on the table, its colour picking up its metallic green, "pleasure doing business with you my man, that makes it thirty five, at this rate I'll be able to retire. Don't worry 'bout paying me back, I'll be rich soon..." he crumpled his eyes in mock confusion, "Or...?"

Clemens laughed again, packing the note in his pocket, and nodded at Halil who had his head slumped over his arms across the table, his eyes letter box open as he hollowly leched at the backside of the woman sitting at the bar on one of the rickety stools. Nick carefully reached over, his forefinger folded behind his thumb, and sharply flicked Halil on the tip of his exposed ear. He sat up with a yelp, rubbing at his smarting extremity, Nick giggling like a whelp, "Wake up you fuckin' sleepy git."

Halil pulled an irritated grimace at Nick, "I'm awake, I'm awake, just taking a break was all." He rocked his head back and peered up at the ceiling, the dulled fuzz of the drug pulling at his temples. He sighed, trying to gather his thoughts and dropped his head forward, throwing a sleep heavy glance at Clemens, who smiled merrily back at him. "So what's going down Clemens, where's the pussy then? I neeed some pussy."

Clemens squinted with confusion, "pussy, what is this pussy you want? I have no pussy."

"The chicks man, chicks, y'know, the frauleins, the fun stuff, the women. Where are they?" Halil hoped that Clemens wouldn't notice the desperation he felt quivering at the back of his throat. He didn't need anything of the sort, just peace of mind, but he didn't want to spoil the party. Nick expelled a mouthful of air, shaking his head, Halil turned to him, "what' s up with you fuckin' little batty boy? I s'pose you want to sit here an' talk about the meaning of life, or eye up my arse or something? Be quiet now. Just be quiet, the men are talking here, you understand you batty boy, the men!" His hand moved swiftly and smoothly through the air, removing Nick's glasses before Nick could react to stop him. He put the glasses to his mouth, misting them with his breath, pulled his shirt out of his trousers and used its end to polish the glasses. When he'd finished he held them up to the light, checking the clarity of the lenses, and perched them deftly back on Nick's nose. "Does that help? Can we see a bit better now? Then take a good look round and tell me if there are any women here?"

"Halil," Nick said in a tone laced with mocking disdain, "we are here to enjoy the dazzling wit and comradeship of three dashing young blades, not to immure ourselves in the sins of the hot and sticky flesh pots to which you are always alluding."

Halil looked at him, licked his lips slowly and methodically, drew in a sharp breath, and said, "Knew it, I fucking knew it all along, fucking bent as pair of Iranian corkscrews you two are." He sipped a fierce little sip of his orange juice, and then nodded his head as if he knew something they couldn't, "yup, a pair of bandy legged poofters you two, trying to get me drugged up, no doubt to lure me off to some back room where some fat bastard is going to roger the fuck out of my poor little arsehole." Wide eyed and in shock he gawked sideways and up at the shape looming toward him, "oh fuck, he's coming, uhh, he's coming here..."He was looking up at the voluminous fat sweating skin bag bearing down upon them, supporting its creaking weight with two thigh like arms shunted down on the tortured table, two brilliant blue glazed eyes burning into Halil's head. Halil looked on terrified as a rivulet of perspiration coursed its way down a glistening forehead and the globe of a hair shorn head creased, breaking in two as the fat man spoke directly to him.

"You are Englander, I think, yes?" Halil slit his eyes as his face folded into a grimace of inscrutability. He shot a questioning glance first at Nick, then at Clemens, but they just both stared blank faced back at him. He ground his teeth. The fuckers. He was sure they'd arranged this little tete â tete. The wankers. He grabbed for the cigarette packet, sticking a camel into the corner of his mouth, trying to look wry and cool and twisting his mouth down at the corners like Robert De Niro while feeling like a wide eyed, sun dazed lizard. Then he looked up sharply as the large hands began to make the table shake as they beat out the rhythm to a song whose name escaped him. Halil felt himself in the unusual position of not knowing what to say, but needing to say something desperately. He realized that

Clemens had noticed his discomfort, and the fact that he was grinning madly didn't help Halil at all.

Then the fat man began to sing. Halil gaped as out of this bleary, bloated face rolled a deep bass, eyelash curling voice Motown and his mum would have been proud of. He shot a smile at Clemens who, without pause, said, "Bernie, you want a joint?"and slid his backside along the wooden bench.

Thus invited and introduced, Bernie, not without a good deal of his belching wheeze, eased his thick thighs and endlessly curving backside into the belittled cubicle, his teasing eyes never leaving Halil for a single second. Then Clemens drew attention to himself by theatrically holding up a finger in the air. Halil looked on bemused as Clemens allowed an unseen joint appear between his lips like some cheap vaudeville magician. Bernie growled a vaudeville chuckle, both he and Nick clapping their hands probably more in anticipation than in appreciation. Halil slumped back onto the table with a whining sigh, realising that this night was not going to be a particularly clear one.

This did not hinder him from taking the smouldering joint which was proudly presented to him by a now wickedly grinning Clemens. But not before Clemens had, between finger and thumb, single handedly flicked open the top of a zippo lighter, which, after clicking the fingers of his other hand, burst into flame, and ignited the elongated and perfumed cigarette. As Halil inhaled deeply, spluttering slightly as he tried to hold onto the raspy, tarred smoke, he felt he could hear the roars and cheers of the rest of the pub applauding their beloved pub wizard, eagerly awaiting another outburst of incomprehensible song from their bulging bard. He turned, heavy lidded, to Nick, glad of his company, feeling they were medieval travellers taking rest in a merry roadside tavern. He wanted to play with the bells on Bernie's red and yellow hat until Nick shook him roughly by the shoulder.

"Wake up mate, gi' us the joint, you nearly fell asleep on the fucking joint. C'mon, wake up a bit here."

Dazed, he opened his eyes to see Nick's hand dancing uncertainly in the air before him, trying to grab the joint wedged between his lips. He moaned slightly as he passed it to him, and turned his heavy head to see Bernie, was it Bernie? slapping the table while singing "She's got a ticket to ride.."his head thrown back, mouth open wide, Clemens by his side tapping the table in time with him. Halil rubbed at his eyes and muttered "the fucking Beatles" through his hash grimed mouth and wondered whether he was going to be able to avoid throwing up.

Bernie brought his head back down and gazed at Halil, nodding his head, his lips tightly pursed as if in serious consideration of Halil's last remark. He placed a clenched fist to his mouth and coughed loudly, his eyebrows raised. He rapped his fingers in a slow roll on the table. He rolled his head carefully around his shoulders, his eyes never once leaving Halil's. Halil came slowly to his senses, feeling worried. "What? What's up? I said something wrong?" Suddenly Bernie's hands broke out in a flurry of movement as they struck out a rhythm on the table and an imagined set of symbols. He spun his sticks effortlessly around his meaty paws, one flying in the air to be smoothly caught and brought down with a sharp sish of the high hat as he broke out into a perfect rendition of "Help."

The three of them looked on dumbfounded. Nick voiced their shared concern, "What the fuck was all that about?"

It was Halil who answered, a small smile of recognition cracking his tired face. "He's playing a drummer, he's a fucking drummer, like Ringo Star."

Bernie's eyes disappeared as he grimaced in disapproval. "Ringo Star was scheiße," he said emphatically, "Pete Best, he was a drummer. Maybe a great drummer. Ringo Star is only playing tin cans. I know." Dismissively he turned to Mac at the bar, putting his hand in the air as if holding a mug of beer to let the barkeeper know he was thirsty. As Mac started to protest Clemens turned as well, and, with a slight nod of his head, let Mac know that he was paying, and, with a twist of his finger over the table, ordered another round. Mac nodded in return and set three long glass beer mugs beneath the taps, sluicing the frothy beer from one to the next, scooping the excess white foam out with a yellowing plastic spatula. His hard eyes flitted expertly across his domain, checking his customers, watching the drinks. The three were oblivious to his deft movements until he arrived, tray balanced effortlessly on one hand, loaded with their golden order,

Apricot Juice and Other Stories...

and another round for the table above them. He handed out the drinks with a grunt of disapproval as Bernie swept his up in his hand and tipped it back without further ado. The others mutely clinked their glasses together with a mutter of a "prost" here, and a "cheers" there.

In the meantime the converstation had progressed something like this:

Halil to Bernie: [Accusing] How the fuck would you know Pete Best was better than Ringo Star...?

Bernie: [Defensive but stubborn] I know. [Sings out loudly, banging the table] I know, I know, I know!

Halil: [Apprehensively] Yeah, but uhh, how d'you know?

Bernie: [Assertively] I was playing with him many years before.

Halil: [Incredulous] You? Who did you play with?

Bernie: [Disdainfully] With Pete Best of course.

Halil: [Pauses to think, and then, triumphantly] You couldn't have played with Peter fucking Best. The Beatles came here round about sixty one. That'd make you at least fifty. No way are you fifty. Naa, you never played with Pete Best. Got you there mate, sorry.

At this point the drinks arrived. After the cheers and the prosts and the clinking of glasses and the supping of beer Bernie turned his by now stern attention back to Halil. Halil felt like simpering, but returned the hard stare swimming in his view. Bernie suddenly laughed a sarcastic bark of a laugh. "The little English boy knows everything. He knows The Beatles, he knows the years, he knows me."

Halil swallowed. He decided flattery was his best bet. "Well, no, I didn't say that did I? I mean like I just meant that you look a bit young for fifty or so, That's all. Honest mate." He looked down at the table, trying to get away from that floodlit gaze, not knowing where to look, to go, to say. He shuddered as a wash of nausea rolled over him. It didn't look like flattery had got him anywhere. He looked for support. "What about you two? Clemens, you've gone strangely quiet on the question of Bernie and the Beatles. What d'you reckon?"

Clemens looked on wisely, gently picked at his left nostril with the little finger of his right hand, and said, "I think, I reckon...? that you are both right and we need another joint to celebrate this." Halil groaned softly, while Bernie grinned happily, as they both watched Clemens laying the little white papers out on the table in readiness. Clemens threw a quick wink of reassurance over to Halil, who looked like he might well have needed it. "Halil, is everything fine with you?" asked Clemens cordially.

"I'm fine, fine. I'm just trying to figure out how I'm going to get through tonight in one piece." answered Halil somewhat wearily, and more truthfully than any of his companions might have thought.

Clemens creased his forehead in mock concern, "Halil my friend, you must not worry that we take you to pieces. I think we are very nice people, yes?" He raised his glass convivially and tapped it against Halil's orange juice. Halil grunted a laugh of agreement and then looked in surprise at the empty seat next to him.

"Where's Nick gone?" he asked quickly, his voice rising, his eyes sweeping the pub feverishly. His last contact with reality had disappeared.

Clemens saved him from the plunge into a disparate world of dreams, and said, "He is at the toilet. Downstairs." Hail wiped a sweaty hand across dry lips and turned back to Bernie who was now in the middle of a perfect, if somewhat deep, rendition of "Help," his hands hammering a resounding beat out of the table. He stopped, hands in midair, as he simultaneously saw Halil watching him and heard Mac shouting his name in remonstration from behind the bar. He attempted placating Mac by bowing his head and patting the air directly in front of him in a gesture of conciliation. After Mac had snarled his approval he turned his attention to Halil, who was looking decidedly worried. "So, you think you know who Bernie played with huh?"

Halil quickly looked away from him and spied with relief his friend, and only contact with the real world, Nick, approaching. This relief slowly flaked to the ground, melting as Nick stopped before arriving at the table, purposely turning his back on Halil, and deliberately engaging in conversation with a bystander.

Appalled at this misconduct, Halil glanced sideways at Bernie, the dreadful realisation that he was going to have to argue his case to an obviously very mad man, burning through his water filled hash haze.

Apricot Juice and Other Stories...

He made the attempt at communication. "Look, if you said you did I'm sure you did, it's just that..." With a sigh he wondered why he always had to be so turnip stupid stubborn as Bernie interrupted him.

"Just what is that? I think you think I am mad or something. Perhaps this is true. But it is also true that I tell you the truth. I am playing with Pete Best in his band. Here in Hamburg. Thank you." He took the joint proffered by Clemens, and sucked in a huge lungful of smoke, theatrically squeezing his eyes shut, puffing out his cheeks like a bullfrog, while holding the heavy smoke in. Then, with a splutter, he exhaled it in a large grey cloud, which cloyed around Halil's head and shoulder's, like a soiled wedding veil.

Halil nodded in caustic appreciation, and then took a sharp intake of breath as he saw Bernie's golden head haloed in the yellow light reflected off the gold painted seat back. He was engulfed in a small religious moment of madness, this Bernie enshrined, and Halil saw, with astounding clarity, the man's mad benignity. Even his anger was acted out for the others. Halil tried pulling himself together once again. Shrugging his shoulders and slurring slightly he said, "Maybe we're all mad, who knows? But look, you and Pete Best, when exactly did you play with him?"

Bernie's face cracked into a golden smile. He slapped the table hard with his one hand and shook the finger of his other hand in Halil's direction. "The Englander is no fool or a mad dog. I play with him in '76 or '77. In a little club on the Kietz, with his band."

"Oh right, in '77," recognition lit up Halil's

voice. At that moment, when it was no longer necessary, Nick decided to return to the table, slumping down next to Halil with a sigh. Halil looked at him suspiciously and tapped him forcibly on his shoulder. "And where the fuck you think you've been eh?"

Before he could answer Bernie had butted in. "It is not where he has been, it is where he goes, that you should ask." Bernie smiled a sagely smile at Halil, who couldn't, despite his momentary insight, return it with the ease it called for.

"Uhh, right," he stammered, unsure where this particular perspective was leading to. He shifted his weight as Nick leant heavily on his arm, more for comfort than for support, and tried to fix Bernie with a good humoured glare. Bernie's attention was, however, now elsewhere, as he raised his fat finger in the air to order another drink. Clemens did likewise, and Nick sighed once again, his head drooping forward. Halil prodded him roughly, "Hey, don't go all fucking melancholy on me now mate."

"It is too early to sleep now," toned in Clemens, seeing Nick's sliding posture. Nick mumbled something into Halil's arm, and then shook himself awake. He looked stonily around the table and, as if affronted, asked, "What's going down?"

Bernie grabbed at the beer floating in the air just above his head, and, in answer to Nick's question, sunk the half litre of amber liquid without blinking. He belched, and gazed wild eyed at Halil. He pointed in his direction, and asked him, "what is your name?"

"Halil," he answered promptly, feeling that this was perhaps too much information.

Bernie mouthed the name silently, as if consuming it to memory, and drummed his heavy fingers on the table, saying "Halil, I must show you something, I show you all something then you know I play with Pete Best."

Halil automatically recoiled at this invitation. "No, no, we believe you, honest, you don't have to show us. It's alright. Clemens, tell the man we believe him."

But Clemens' interest had been aroused. Halil let out a small cry of astonishment as the man leant over to Bernie and asked, "what is it you have to show?"

Halil saw Bernie's bulbous features twitch and rattily narrow as he realised he had a captive audience. He saw that the yellow halo was the cheap light bouncing off the sheen of sweat greasily coating Bernie's brow. He sucked hard on his cigarette and tried to rouse support from Nick. Nick grinned vacantly in reply, and punched him on the arm in a sign of everlasting comradeship. It was Halil's turn to sigh.

Meanwhile Bernie had been germanely conversing with Clemens. Clemens turned to Halil. "We must go to his place and see."

"What must we see?" asked Halil caustically.

"He says it is a surprise, but it is something given by The Beatles to this Pete Best, which he gave to Bernie. Bernie say we must see it. Come we go. It is fine."Clemens took a long swig from his beer and

Apricot Juice and Other Stories...

looked encouragingly at Halil. Seeing the alcoholic glaze pasted across his face did nothing to encourage Halil. He wished that his head would clear.

Then Nick started to wake up, stretching and yawning, his arms reaching and waving around in the air. "Alright, let's hit it," he proclaimed to all and sundry, rising and tugging at the sleeves of his jacket. Halil looked at him in distress, trying to motion him with peculiar eye movements and grimaces to sit back down. Nick frowned at him. "C'mon, let's get out of here. Make a move, it can't be worse than here."

"I'm fine here, it's great here. We don't have to go anywhere," rising panic mewled in Halil's voice. But Nick, Clemens and Bernie were now moving with the surety of decision. He saw there was no way out of this particular situation. In resignation he started pulling at his coat upon which he was sitting, and, with utter dismay hanging heavily on the corners of his mouth, heard it tear on the nail head upon which it was snagged. "Fer fuck's sake," he cried as he inspected the fray of the blue lining. He wanted to complain to the others, to Nick, but they were half down the bar, negotiating payment. He slipped his arms into the coat, shrugging it onto his shoulders and rubbed tiredly at his eyes. He walked over to stand behind Nick, who looked over his shoulder at him, oblivious to Halil's little disaster with the jacket.

"What's up with you now. C'mon, it'll be a laugh, we're just going to go up to his place," intoned Nick. Halil grimaced, the leery faces of his companions bobbing uncertainly before him. He lurched a step forward as Bernie slapped him heavy handed on the back of his shoulder, and suddenly had the image of a jolly Bavarian in lederhosen, and nearly retched at the idea of Bernie bound up in those German leather hotpants.

"Come Englishman, we go to me, I show you I play with Pete Best," rattled out Bernie in one gasping, beer laden breath, as he stuck his pasty mien into Halil's face. Halil turned away, sticking his hand out to the bar, seeking moral support. The other three, already finished with the business of paying, were headed for the door, Clemens already out on the street. Realising that they were probably too drunk and too stoned to even consider waiting, Halil, with a rising sense of foreboding, hurried after them.

The air outside was cooler than before, and Halil felt an involuntary shiver whisper its way down his back. He twitched his shoulders and blinked his eyes as he turned the corner, following the flapping of Clemens' incongruously long overcoat. From behind, the three made an odd pack, with the compact Nick being threatened on the one side by the overhanging Clemens, and pressed in on the other by the bulging Bernie. In the dark of the street's cool evening shadows Halil saw a deformed malignity to their gait as they traipsed along like three old London ghouls. The fat one turned to him, his eyes glinting hollowly in the yellow brown street lamp, and gestured with one arm to follow. Halil, his brow a little sweated, wanted to grab Nick and run, but, with a quick pull at his stomach, realised he was panic bound to following these three to the mad Bernie's house.

He almost ran into them as they had stopped in front of one of the old weathered houses, all three looking up at the dimly lit, blackened, flaking facade. Bernie fumbled in his trouser pocket, pulling out a thick, jangling set of keys and a snot smeared handkerchief which he dabbed at his nose and thrust back into his pocket. He climbed the cracked concrete steps to the front door and waggled a key in the lock until the door opened with a creak and a crack of old blistered wood. His face hooded in the dark of the hallway, he beckoned the others up the steps with a crooked finger.

Halil put a hand on a cold stone wall, suddenly removing it hastily and falling up the steps as the icy wall slowly pushed back. A light clicked on in the hallway, illuminating the stench of urine wrinkling Halil's nose. He managed a weak smile as Nick pulled a face at him, pointing at the damp flecked walls, streaked with the depressing yellow brown of rusty water. Halil clenched his fist and began to grind his teeth together as he saw Bernie and Clemens already standing at the open, peeling door to what was obviously Bernie's flat. He almost turned back when he saw a small, mustard coloured pool of drying vomit, but he knew he had no choice. Swallowing hard against the gut wrenching smell, he rushed on by, ushered into the gloomy flat by a small push in the back from an over eager Bernie. Halil, moving quickly away from the hand, stumbled over what he took to be a stool, into what might have once been the living room. He stared helplessly around him, into the darkness, and then blinked furiously, one hand held up to his eyes for protection as Bernie switched on the single cold, yellow lightbulb, hanging forlornly from the centre of the room.

"Fucking hell," exploded Nick as he walked into the room with Clemens at his side, followed closely by Bernie. "What is all this?" he demanded of Bernie.

Bernie hung his head to one side, chewing a little on his lower lip. "Sorry, I do not have much visitors here." He reached over to grab at a plate, half-filled with encrusted soup, furred with small fluffs of fungi. But neither Nick, nor the others, had seen this. All over the room, stacked thigh to shoulder high in every corner, were piles of records. Halil now saw that the stool he had fallen over was, in reality, a small table of records which had fanned out and spilled over the uncarpeted floor. At one end, he saw that someone had obviously been just as clumsy, as two piles had toppled over against each other, some of the black discs having slipped out of their covers, hanging on precariously to this man-made precipice. The windows were obscured by records. There was no space for chairs, or a sofa, or a table. In the middle of one wall was a record player, the speakers perched at either end of the room, each placed on top of a pile of records. Halil carefully crouched down to look at the old record player, with its long silver spindle, and black plastic hook for stacking forty fives. He almost moaned when he saw that the playing head had been broken clean off the tracking arm, and hung there loosely, like a broken hand, connected only by two wires. He looked around at the records and then up at Bernie.

But Bernie, and the others, were no longer there. Halil stood up with a start, almost knocking over the stack of records next to him, a flash of fear biting coldly at his chest. He negotiated his way through to the doorway, but realised that it led to the staircase outside. Suddenly, he heard Nick calling him from somewhere to his left. He looked in that direction, and, through a gap between the records, he saw a second door in the wall. He tentatively started making his way towards it when, with a small pop, the light went out. Halil froze, wanting to scream. A faint "help" dribbled from his lips as he felt the records towering above him, looming over him, leaning down upon him. Instinctively, he began to slowly crouch down, seeking the comfort of the cold floorboards. He began to sweat feverishly, the clammy sheen coating his skin, making him shiver. Looking at the floor he heard a click of a light switch and saw a pale, yellow path of light spread out from behind the pillar of records standing to his side. He edged his way slowly towards this, almost crawling along. As he entered the pale pathway a shadow loomed over him.

"What do you do down there?" bellowed Bernie, standing over him. "Come here, I show you some-thing." Halil slowly rose as Bernie waddled down the grimy passageway to another room at the end. Nick and

Clemens were waiting there. Halil noticed that Bernie had something long and cylindrical in his hand, but couldn't make out what it was.

He gritted his teeth, his hands cold with angst, and followed Bernie into what turned out to be a kitchen. Its floor had the same wooden floorboards as the living room, its walls a grotty grey-white, the once white kitchen tiles above the little two ring cooker and the tin wash basin smeared brown with old grease. At the back there was a door which leant open onto the balcony obscured in darkness. Still shivering, he walked out into the darkness, vaguely hearing Clemens and Nick's concerned tones aimed at him, but not answering.

As the cool evening air stroked his face, he felt the cold of the hospital walls slice through his body. As he saw Bernie's thick hands manipulate the cylinder, turning it slowly around to show a long white taper, he saw the hands of the woman as they snaked toward him. As the lighter in Bernie's other hand burst into a yellow flame, illuminating the cold glare in the man's eyes, Halil saw the steely glaze of her eyes, as her nails scraped at the window between them. He heard a fizz as the taper caught light, and, in the glow, saw the cylinder which the manically laughing Bernie was holding in his hand. He screamed, turning, pushing, stumbling, running, the shouts and thumps of the others following behind him, he crashed through one pile of records, sending black discs spinning through the air, grasping for the front door, sliding in the sick, careening down the stairs, aware that Nick and Clemens were at his heels. As they bundled out onto the street both Nick and Clemens laid their hands on his shoulders, "What's up, what's up?" repeated Nick, concerned and out of breath.

Halil looked at both of them, first the one then the other, his heaving chest singing in is ears. "Didn't you see what it was?" he asked.

"Sure," said Clemens, "it was a firework."

"A firework?" asked Halil uncertainly, his eyes wide with shock, his body shaking, his face pale and awash with running sweat.

"Yeah, a firework. I think it was supposed to be a present from Pete Best," said Nick, starting to laugh.

Clemens butted in, "no, I think it was another Pete, they used to play together, but he died last year. Bernie never knew Pete Best, or the Beatles. He was confused, or making it up. It was just a normal firework."

"Oh fuck. I thought it was fucking dynamite. I saw a stick of fucking dynamite. I thought it was a bomb. I thought I was goin' to die..." Halil's eyes ran recklessly back and forth between the two, but he began to relax, his body heaving with his sobs, as Nick took him in his arms, Clemens rubbing his back, both of them muttering and whispering little words of encouragement into his ears.

Upstairs on his balcony stood Bernie, his vision clouded with tears, shouting after the others, "wait, wait...," seeing the broken mountain of records in his living room. He turned back to the now spitting tube standing on the floor and took a sharp step back as it threw out a high fountain of bright, violet flame. At its apex, in the whorls of cascading colour, where the sparks slowly turned and floated to the ground, through the fog of his tear washed eyes Bernie could make out, in a burning red, the words "The Beatles." A laugh broke through his distress, and, with certainty, he proclaimed, "Pete was the best."

FIGHTS AND FAKIRS IN CAFÉ O

It's always a little dim in Café Oriental, but on this particular day the clouds were hanging low, the daylight was dusky, and in the café it was positively dark. The two young men huddled over the obligatory candle as if it were the last glowing log of their camp fire and the cold of the night was threatening to encase them. Nick coughed gutturally through the greying cloud of his cigarette, took a bitter sip at his sparkling wine, and looked meanly into the dark eyes of his companion.

"Fucking load of hippy shit if you ask me," said Nick decisively. His companion nodded his head in agreement and grabbed at the neck of the blue labelled, green bottle standing between them, pouring the prickling liquid into his thin stemmed glass. He sniffed loudly, his fingers, chipped and gnarled, delicately clasping the stem, and lifting it to his lips. Nick watched him carefully, until his friend caught his eye, blinked in apology, and clinked his glass against Nick's.

"I guess they got too much money or something." His voice had the nasal twang of a North American accent, but the uneven cut of his diction revealed that English was not his native language. "Look here," he said neutrally as he slid a leaflet over to Nick, his index finger pointing to one of the paragraphs. Nick took it casually, flipping the leaflet open with a flick of his hand.

"They must be fucking loaded," spat Nick, gesturing rudely at the pamphlet with his thumb. His hands were neither chipped nor gnarled, but thin, and finely veined, the skin smooth and unblemished. "Eight hundred marks for...let's see...a day's meditation, guided by your own personal guru...," he said, translating from the German, it not occurring to him that his friend could understand it anyway. He threw the leaflet down in disgust. "Personal fucking guru, my arse, I bet I could be a better bloody personal guru than any of those...," he stopped mid-sentence, searching for an appropriate word, his finger jabbing at the leaflet. His face suddenly broke into a smile. "Hey Marten, that's it. Fuck it, all we got to do is some guruing and we'll be made."

Marten snorted a laugh through his nose. The image of him and Nick as New Age gurus floated through his head, Nick with a turban which kept unravelling, one end swinging defiantly before his nose. He, of course, would be robed in black, and turbanless, his dark black hair grown long and melting into his cloak, starkly contrasting the white streak, inherited from his mother, which ran slightly left of centre through his mane. Marten was not only vain, he also had a penchant for little visual clichés in which he, more often than not, starred. The café once more refilling his vision, he saw Nick staring bemusedly at him. He realised he still had an awkward little giggle left over in his mouth. He let it out with a surreptitious little cough as if he were laughing during a church sermon.

Nick pulled a face and slid his glasses professorially down his nose. "It wasn't that funny," he said dryly.

"I wasn't laughing," lied Marten idly. Nick didn't bother objecting. He was still musing over the contents of the leaflet, with titles such as "Three days of Transcendental Meditation" and "A seminar toward living in harmony with others," punctuated with pictures of several thin, sun-browned, straggly haired men, some of European, some of Asian origin. All shared the same open eyed, warm hearted, sincere, corporate smile, and similar off-white, baggy trousers with matching formless linen jackets. Nick knew that the same sect which printed the leaflet also ran the pub, and had decorated it accordingly. The walls were hand painted in a browning crimson, with rows of delicately faded petals, edged in black and peach. Hanging from the ceiling were several small copper lanterns, these threw off a dim light through a myriad of star and crescent shapes cut into the metal. Or there were the tasselled chandeliers, one constructed of tiny, shiny whelk shells, one of rusty, old, inverted oriental oil lamps, with bulbs suspended from the upturned spouts. The light from these glanced wetly off the bronze coloured tables, with strange hieroglyphic twists cut symmetrically into the surface. There was a small arch cut into the wall, dividing the café into two, which served as a window between the two rooms. This was somewhat unnecessary given that a six foot wide opening had been cut through the same wall. The room into which it opened into, and in which Nick and Marten sat, ended in a massive wall mirror reflecting the whole dark entourage back onto itself, and was lined with benches carpeted with Indian rugs. Wafting over this rich entourage of furniture was the constant fragrance of burnt herbs, twisting up into the air from strategically placed joss sticks.

The bar was in the other room, through the opening in the wall, and down a step. This was partially cordoned off by a mahogany coloured banister, which was no doubt meant to give the single step the effect of a stage or a balcony, but failed in its intention. This imaginary balcony looked across at the mahogany coloured, two tiered bar, the second level high enough to obscure the heads of both bar staff and customer. This meant that nearly all transactions took place across the low-set swing door, which led behind the bar to where the bar staff would hover. Here they would wait until the last inexorable minute when, after innumerable winks, waves and shouts they had to leave the safety of their busy little bunker, and walk through that swinging door to serve the customers. Payment was never made at the tables, always at that little door.

In direct contrast to the strumming vibes of peacefulness supposedly emanating from the café's oriental ambience, the bar staff tended to be both wary and brusque, their eyes flitting suspiciously around the rooms. This was no doubt due to the owner's ruling that no-one should be excluded from the establishment, all ways of life should be tolerated, ignoring the fact that not all varieties of life are tolerable. The people who came here, a mix of student high life and social low life, came not for spiritual enlightenment, but for spiritual sedation, it being a favoured place for the buying and trying of all sorts of substances. This atmosphere of lawful laxity was always laced with an authentic spice of danger, since the dealers plying their wares did not feel obliged to hang in doorways and lounge hidden in toilets, and so mingled and socialised with a basically unsuspecting, if not naive, clientele.

Nick and Marten thought they were spared such pleasantries through a little daytime, rather than evening, drinking. Nick eyed his glass, idly considering his discovery that his alcohol consumption had very little to do with his free will, but had a direct correlation to the available drinking time. He was on the verge of worrying that his days were merging undefinably into the nights, the only common denominators being drink and drunkenness. He contemplated his glass again, swilling the faintly hissing white wine around, until a small head of foam crusted the liquid. He felt like a bohemian as he stared, trance-like, at the effervescing bubbles backgrounded by tassels and copper twists, and then thought that he might well just be drunk.

Marten was steeped in a wine soaked meditation of his fingernails, taking a corner of card he had torn from the cheaply printed drinks menu, and sliding it carefully beneath the dirty crescents until they had been scraped clean. At the same time, he was wondering whether he should travel to Spain with Nick. His eyes trawled over Nick, who was staring into his glass, and he wondered whether it would be the same as this in

Spain. Satisfied with his nails, Marten leant over and tapped Nick on the shoulder and, his voice deepening with seriousness, said "with Spain, I don't want to hang around getting pissed and stoned all the time, understand? I want to see some things, you know?"

Nick eyed him carefully. "You want some culture, is that what you mean?" he said with a taint of disdain, the sarcastic twist of his mouth distorting the word "culture." Marten raised his hand in objection to Nick's tone, but Nick carried on, a little friendlier now, "it's alright, it's alright. Look, I got it figured. Mornings we do the sightseeing, afternoons we do the beach, and evenings we take what comes, no problem. A bit of culture 'll do me good. Don't worry, it'll be a laugh."

Marten smiled distantly at Nick. "I'm not worried," he said off-handedly. He was about to carry on when both turned toward the door as a woman burst in shouting. She was tall, and was clothed in tight fitting, black pants and a sleeveless, billowed cream blouse, its seams lined with a tickling frill. The bones of her face, and the cut of her body, too square and angular to say she was pretty, but she retained a high nosed, handsome quality as she strode furiously into the bar. Her straight, waist length hair was dyed to a silky blond which frayed out into a fronded fan as she span round to confront a stocky young man, the mahogany skin of his expressionless face, soft and smooth, hardly betraying the jealous anger screaming loud and vividly from his eyes. He was dressed in the familiar black cotton, baggy suit of the Romany criminal class, his greasy black   rings of hair cresting the greying collar of his jacket. He thrust out his arm, a thick gold bracelet, a chunkily glinting cliché, peeping from his sleeve, and grabbed at her bared arm. She slapped his hand away, painful red flowers of pressed flesh marking where his hand had been, but, although her pale grey eyes were hot and shiny with fear and rage, her skin clung tightly to its pallid hue as if refusing any part in this emotional outrage. She had been backing away from the man all this time when, suddenly, she planted her feet in the ground and stood him off square. Legs apart, hands on hips, she leant forward from her waist, her face thrust in his, and bawled, "you're a fucking arsehole Charlie, you hear me, a bastard good-for-nothing arsehole. Just fuck off and leave me alone," or words to that effect.

The young man was plainly affronted, but was unsure how to respond to this outburst. He looked at her haughtily, and then clicked his fingers and pointed at the door with his thumb, his voice hoarse with emotion as he said, "come, outside, now!"

The man called Charlie made another lunge for her, but she swiftly backed out of range, now hysterically screaming, "get out, get out, leave me alone..." Nick dropped his head onto his arms folded across the table, and looked sheepishly up at Marten who rolled back his eyes in sympathy.

Suddenly, Marten took a sharp breath, staring incredulously at the scene unrolling before them. A spindly, stubbled man, somewhere in his late twenties, or early thirties, with a thin, drug chiselled face framing the slow moving, pain dulled eyes of the inarticulate, and wispy flyaway brown-blond hair, rose from the bar, at which he had been sitting unobserved during the whole course of events, in order to intervene. Seeing him, an old man's chequered sports jacket hanging loosely from his skinny shoulders, his cheap white jeans a cut too small, his flapping plastic trainers, and the brave intent glaring from his face, Nick swore volubly, "oh fer fuck's sake."

Time slowed down. The man had stood up and placed himself at Charlie's shoulder, who was now pointing and shouting at the woman, "you dirty two-faced bitch, how much of my money goes through your nose, how much of my money have you smoked? You dirty little junkie slut, how many of my friends have you fucked on my drugs? You come with me now, else you'll pay, everything, everything!"

She flinched and ducked as he raised his arm, shouting and sobbing, "I don't understand, I can't fucking understand you..." This was explained by the fact that he had been shouting at her in Yugoslavian and no-one in the café was any the wiser as to what was going on.

Marten pulled a twisted face at Nick as they saw the man standing at Charlie's shoulder grab at his raised arm, holding it back with the gallantry laden words, "leave the lady alone." Both Nick and Marten saw the heat rising to Charlie's face, he stood stock still, taking a second to digest this outrage, his arm still hanging in the air. Grating his teeth in a dog like snarl, he span round, wrenching his arm free from the man's grip, both his hands curling around the man's throat, both thumbs pressing against the larynx, the Adam's apple bobbling out under the pressure. He lifted the man off his feet, the man's hands clawing at his, the woman at his back shouting in his ear, pulling at his hair, "get off him. Charlie, leave him alone, get off him." He stared at the man's face, half in a trance, half as if studying it, waiting for the right moment. Seeing the fear in the man's wide eyes, he felt his rage settling, leaving him cold, an icy maliciousness coursing through him, freeing him from the choking bands of his anger. He squeezed a little tighter, watched as the man's eyes began to roll back, white in their sockets, ignored the bird beak stabs of irritating pain as the woman pulled at his hair. He waited until the man's clawing grew weaker, a feeble slapping at his arms, and, as if he were protesting his innocence, opened his hands, widening his arms as a man shows he is without a weapon, or as a man who is about to embrace the head of his son and bestow a kiss upon him, and watched his assailant fall limply to the ground, gagging and coughing for breath.

Feeling the yanking at his head he ponderously turned, plucking the woman's hands from his hair, and roughly thrusting her away from him, he balled his hand into a fist, a thick gold signet ring gleaming viciously on his middle finger, turned his fist with the closed palm facing upwards, and sliced the edge of the ring into her face just beneath her eye. He watched, an expression of neutral disregard upon his face, as she fell back with a cry, grabbing at the bar for support, a crimson tear peeling down her cheek. The waitress was stridently shouting at him to get out. With a snort and an arrogant flick of his mane he turned his back on her to leave the bar. The man he had left lying on the ground had got to his feet. He pointed his forefinger at him, and, with the same hand, slapped him loudly across the face and strode out of the door. All the while, the dulcet tones of Lennon and McCartney singing "Let it be" had been droning out from the stereo.

Nick and Marten exchanged taut faced glances, the twist of their eyes betraying both fear and relief. Marten's hands were both balled into white knuckled fists, Nick was grinding his teeth while playing nervously with a ring, running it through his fingers. It fell to the table with a clatter, and the man who had just been slapped looked over at the two accusingly. The woman was dabbing at her face with a tissue given to her by the waitress, holding it to the wound, and then taking it away, only to feel the warm blood coalesce in the cut, and slowly trickle down her cheek, so that she had to once more raise the reddened tissue. She looked over to the man who had tried to assist her and placed her free hand on his shoulder, squeezing it gently. She smiled sympathetically, and said, "thanks for helping. He's a real bastard that one, you want to be careful." She winced theatrically as she put the tissue back to her bleeding cut, and then inspected the blood on the tissue. "It's still bleeding," she said uselessly.

The waitress came round from the other side of

the bar, and began to hover in front of the two, trying to get a good look at the cut. "Let me see a minute," she wheedled, and fussed around the woman, her hands flapping at her face.

The woman took a step back, flustered. "Is it bad?" she asked, concerned, dabbing almost obsessively at the cut. Both the waitress and the man leant forward to check. The waitress tactfully and gently pried the woman's hand away from her face. The blood welled up again in the wound, and began to run down her cheek.

Although it was only a little nick, the slow swelling at its edges showed that it was deep. The waitress, despite her own hammering heart, tried to calm the woman down by holding onto her hand, and consequently found herself dabbing uselessly at the wound. "I don't think it'll scar, but you should go to hospital. I think it needs a stitch." The waitress felt a little mean saying this. It was not what she thought. But she'd caught a glance of Charlie, gait aggressively posed, pacing up and down outside in the square. She was terrified that he would return and really lay into the woman. She had a quarter of an hour until Hassan turned up to take over from her shift, and she was praying that, just for once, he would be early, or at least on time. She noticed that her dabbing hand was trembling, and gulped in a large mouthful of air to steady herself. The woman was talking a ream of incessant gibberish about Charlie and being marked for life, and, seeing her wide-eyed glaze, the waitress wondered guiltily if the woman was high and not scared.

Oblivious to the waitress's deliberations, the woman and the man who had so gallantly defended her honour had now moved on from complaints to exchanging gratitudes, compliments, and declinations. This went on until the man reached for a pad and a pen and wrote down both name and number, passing the scrap of paper to the woman, who took it with a smile and a swing of her long hair. She inspected the lettering and mouthed the man's name. "Nils," she said softly.

Listening to this conversation, the waitress had taken a step back from the two. Her earlier suspicion had turned to outright exasperation, which was by now shared by Nick and Marten, who had been watching the scene the whole of the time, but far enough away to be engaged in a separate set of unfolding emotions.

Nick was frozen to his seat by the icy indecision of the physical coward. The scene had rapidly drained his body of all vestiges of movement or motivation. He had sat there helplessly, a debilitating sarcastic anger directed, not at the sequence of events rolled out before him, but at the fright shivered, thin armed boy he perceived himself to be. This was not true, of course. He was compactly built, with powerful hunched shoulders, but this abstract knowledge did nothing to assuage either his fear, or his anger. These two danced a tumultuous whirlwind throughout his body, quivering between fight and flight, until the point where he was ready to pound his tightly clenched fists against his bowed head.

Marten, in contrast to Nick, was not susceptible to this adrenalin induced paralysis. As the shouting began, his stomach had lurched, he had grown bright eyed and excited, his breath quickening in his nostrils, the puffy gossamer web of alcohol eaten away as he leant forward to see more clearly. Then, as the situation diffused, his excitement dampened to a dull, throbbing headache of annoyance and irritation at the inconclusive anticlimax. He turned bitterly to his friend, inwardly cursing the pathetically cheap life of the district he lived in. "Fucking junkies, they should take their shit somewhere else," he muttered disparagingly, his heavy brows knitted, darkly cresting his frustrated expression of distaste. He snatched at the thin glass and emptied it with a single swig as he watched the man and waitress fussing like flies around the woman's minuscule cut.

Nick, plagued by other thoughts, and wrapped in confusion, was already on his feet and moving belatedly in their direction. He halted midway as he saw the man rising, an agreement among the three obviously having been reached. He heard the man solicitously saying, "I'll take you to the underground, you can go to the hospital in St. Georg." This was not what stopped Nick in his tracks, however. It was the look of disdain quickly thrown at him by the man. It sliced through him, a damning indictment passed with the hollow wooden slap of a gavel. Nick stared and sighed as the man took the woman's proffered arm, and escorted her, like a gentleman, out of the door.

The waitress, built slight and pert, her head

crowned with bubbled curls of short, wavy, mouse brown hair, heard Nick's sigh and smiled openly at him in sympathy. "I hope he doesn't come back, or there'll be real trouble."

Nick, caught by the light dancing in the eyes of her smile, warmed instantly to her and felt his face, his body, break out in a heart melting beam. But the face of the waitress had already hardened into a knowing indifference as she turned away, busy with cups and saucers and a cloth, leaving him standing, smiling stupidly into thin air. His buoyant demeanour rapidly evaporated into a beacon of red embarrassment. Vaguely he realised that smiling at customers was just another part of her job, and wiped a hand across his glowing forehead. He turned uncertainly back to Marten, who raised his eyebrows in an offhand manner. Then he grabbed the bottle and waved it at Nick who nodded in compliance. He turned back to the waitress. "'S'cuse, can we have another bottle of..." but she had already seen the gesture, had a bottle of sparkling wine in her hand, and was unfurling the blue tinsel foil from the bottle's white plastic cork. She prised the cork off carefully, but, even so, it spouted a little head of froth which dribbled down the side of the green bottle. Without comment, she passed the bottle to Nick, who sullenly took it, and, without a word, returned to the table at which Marten was sitting, idly tracing its metallic grooves with a dirty thumbnail.

"Have they gone?" asked Marten, somewhat superfluously since he had seen them go out of the

Apricot Juice and Other Stories...

door. Nick tutted in simultaneous rebuke and affirmation. "Good, it's getting so that you can't have a drink anywhere in the square." He snatched at the bottle and let it gush into the glass, swearing loudly as it foamed up over the sides, leaving a little pool of wasted wine shimmering on the metal table top. He pushed the liquid around with his forefinger, and then wiped it vigorously back and forth on the leg of his black jeans. The two looked at each other surreptitiously, and then once more gently chimed their glasses together with a little chink, and a nod of the head, as if they were a pair of corrupted old politicians, drinking to the ill health of the town's new mayor.

Nick turned round as he saw Marten start, and heard the café door swing shut with a bang. It was Charlie again. The waitress didn't wait for him to say anything, just began baying at him to get out. Both Nick and Marten rose to their feet as he grabbed her arm and pulled him to her. He flustered something viciously in her ear and then strode out of the door. The hesitantly approaching Nick thought it was fortunate that Charlie hadn't turned round to see the two of them coming.

As they reached her, all in a matter of seconds, Marten noted that the waitress was both pretty, especially with her brown green eyes, wide and darting through fear, and had turned an almost translucent white. He bunched down so that he was lower than she, his elbows resting on the bar, and looked slightly upwards at her. "What did he say? Are you alright?"

Her racing eyes slowly came to rest on his, she swallowed once, and tried to answer, but her throat just creaked like an old wooden door. Marten waited patiently as she coughed and then took a sip of water from a glass standing ready for such occasions, coughed again, and tried once more. "Mad bastard," she stammered, but her voice was already gaining strength as indignation began to course through her. "Bastard threatened to cut my tongue off if I rang the police." She shook her head, and wrinkled up her nose, as if she had just drank a foul tasting cough medicine, while Marten nodded in a cool, but interested, sympathy. "What do you think I should do?" she asked him confidentially, roping him into the little circle of her sphere of intimacy.

Marten smirked inwardly, but felt slightly exasperated as he sensed Nick's hovering presence at his back. He looked hard at the waitress, and then offered a comforting smile. "Phone the police. He won't do anything," he said in a tone of shared conspiracy. Then he ground his teeth together, looking round annoyed, as Nick sighed loudly behind him. Nick beamed at him, and then rolled his eyes back in his head while Marten glowered.

Suddenly, their little tryst was rudely interrupted as the café door swang open. Nick jumped a little in the air, and then swore, seeing that it was only the would-be hero from earlier. He nodded at the three who were staring at him, the girl with her mouth wide open, as if she were drawn in a comic book. Then he raised his empty bottle, which had been standing there alone all this time, and signalled to the waitress that he was ready for another.

She looked anxiously toward Marten, who merely shrugged his shoulders, and coldly turned his back on her, marching back toward his table, grabbing at Nick's arm on his way, pulling him along, even though he was more than willing to sit back down. They heard the waitress trying to reason with the man. "Wouldn't it be better if you just went home now? I don't want any more trouble..."

But the man wasn't even slightly interested in her proposal. He stuck his jaw out obstinately, and then rubbed at his chin in an arrogant gesture of haughtiness. "I'm not frightened," he sneered, "I came in here to have a beer and that's what I'm going to do." The girl saw from his look that there was no use in arguing, and, with a twist of her wrist, flipped the metal top off the head of a green beer bottle. She passed it to him without uttering a word, and returned to washing and wiping the dirty glasses. He perched on his stool, crouched over the beer, his hands held around the bottle as if it was providing them with warmth. His lips were pursed stiff and slender, as if he were determined to carry out a difficult undertaking.

The waitress kept throwing waited looks over at the man, interspersed with anxious glances at her watch. Hassan was late, and, for her, this was no day for being late. Her forehead crumpled, and she closed her eyes, as a dismal pressure welled up at the back of her head. She gritted her teeth together and rubbed harder at the glass she was drying, half hoping it would break in her hand so that she could ask someone for help.

She turned around sharply as the café door creaked open, and, despite her miserable mood, she couldn't help smiling as Hassan's long body bound in through the door, his mouth twisted apologetically, his dark, shadow rimmed eyes opened in appeal. He loped up to the bar in a few long strides and kissed the waitress on both cheeks. "Ahh Anna," he crooned, his voice soft and purring, "I'm sorry I'm late. Been busy today?" he asked collegially. She looked up at him, and, as he saw the edge of her mouth begin to flutter, he realised that something was wrong. He automatically and incorrectly assumed that he was the cause. "I'm really sorry 'bout being late," he pined. "If you've got to go, I'll clear up." He tried a small cheeky smile and a duck of his gangly body so he could look her straight in the eye. It usually worked.

She waved a hand limply in the air, as if to brush him away. "No. It's no problem. We had trouble earlier with Charlie and that girl who always hangs 'round him..."

"Charlotte," he filled in quickly.

"Yeah, maybe, I don't know her, but the stupid bastard hit her, and then threatened a customer." She nodded in the man's direction, Hassan looking casually over his shoulder at him. "And then he threatened to cut my tongue out if I said anything." She let out a caustic little laugh and sniffed.

Hassan looked at her impassively, and simply raised his eyebrows, their long thin arches forming two simultaneous question and exclamation marks. He pondered the situation for a second, and then asked, "But you're alright, he didn't do anything to you?" His voice had dropped in volume and pitch to emphasise his grasp of the obvious gravity of the affair, but he was actually wondering whether she would let him nip out and grab something to eat. He ran a hungry hand over his stiff, black, wiry hair, then shot both hands to the back of his head to fiddle with the band bunching his hair into a tight little stubby tail. His long young face, with its childish skin, remained deadpan, helped by the couple of grains of brown powder he had earlier rubbed into his gums to keep him going through his shift. His sparsity of expression was betrayed by the darting friendliness of his eyes, up to now untouched by the drug. With an effort, he creased his face into a look of concern, and, with a taint of the plea in his voice, said, "look, do you mind waiting a minute, I've got to eat..."

Anna sighed dramatically, even though she knew, and he knew, that she had to cash up her takings before he could start. But she had suffered, and, like most, had never understood what people had against sharing when it came to suffering. Hassan accordingly winced, and was suitably repaid for taking his share of the burden. "OK, but be quick, I want to get out of here." She watched as, with a twirl and a few long strides, he flew out of the door. She pulled a face, took the large black purse out of her waistband, and began counting its contents.

He returned before she had finished her calculations, balancing the drinks written down on little slips of paper against the money in her purse. This was a fiddly process, which was both annoying and added financial risk since all losses incurred were subtracted from the tips. Of course, it could work both ways, Anna thought to herself as she slipped a fifty-mark note into her pocket, crumpling up two of the accompanying slips of paper. The owner had neither invested in a cash-till, nor did he pay enough wages to hinder that sort of thing. All his employees had at some stage reached the conclusion, some together, some alone, that their own form of value-added tax, as long as it was not too high and regularly applied, would go unnoticed, falling as it did under the normal running costs of a café.

Hassan, his cheeks bulging out with chewed food, raised his eyebrows wryly as he saw her place the note in her pocket. She caught his look and immediately flushed, uncertain whether Hassan would reprimand her. The corners of his food filled mouth twitched into a little smirk, and he winked in acknowledgement. She looked down at the purse, packing it away. She turned her back on Hassan, checked that everything was cleared up, and bent down to pick up her faded blue anorak lying under the counter. She shrugged it onto her shoulders and squeezed carefully passed Hassan, her buttocks brushing against his, while he was still munching away at his food, a Turkish pizza from the snack bar next door. He looked back as Anna turned and waved goodbye to him. He held the rest of the rolled over pizza up in the air to wish her farewell, and then stuffed it quickly into his mouth. He scanned the café quickly, but there were just the three, the man at the bar whom he didn't know, and the two at the table. He recognised both but could put no names to the faces. One of them peered at him, and lifted his glass as if he were raising a toast to Hassan. Hassan turned away and pulled out his black waiter's purse, checking its contents swiftly with his fingertips.

The man sitting at the bar wiped a thin knobbly hand through his thin hair. He tapped his bottle on the counter top to attract Hassan's attention. He in turn, leant over the counter without a word, in order to establish the make of beer. Again without a word, he reached down into the fridge under the counter, and passed the man the appropriate bottle. The man took it from him without a murmur. Both had recognised that he wanted to drink and not talk.

Hassan grabbed at a damp dishcloth, walked out into the café, and began wiping down the tables, despite them being clean. He wandered past Nick and Marten, who were engrossed in conversation. He noted with a passing interest that they were speaking English, but too fast for him to follow.

Nick was on a monologue: "That's why I came here. It got too fucking hairy in London. Like this mate of Mike's, I didn't know him but I knew the other guy who was in the car with him, well they were just driving along and he sees another guy in a car who owes him money, and follows him and tries to get him to stop. Mike said it was four hundred quid that was all." He paused, taking a gulp of sparkling wine, grimacing because his heart burn was beginning to bite. He went on. "Any way the guy they were following, apparently he thought they were another gang, he didn't recognise them, stops, gets out the car and shoots the one guy dead. The guy I knew, the other one in the car, he gets shot in the arm. That was too fucking heavy for me I had to get out of it. And like Mike was just dealing hash and tabs when I moved in, that was OK, great time like, but then he got into coke and they started doing crack at the weekends...And you got some fucking weird types in the flat, like some really heavy criminal bastards, so I was glad to get out and get over here..."

All three were suddenly interrupted in their respective occupations of talking, listening and wiping, as a crash and a cry came from the region of the bar. All three threw their stares in that direction to witness the man called Nils lying crumpled in a jerking ball on the dirty floor. His body appeared to hop of its own accord, first in one direction, then in the other. Nick could make out the lined contortions of his face accompanying each cry as Charlie kicked him in the stomach, once sharply in the head, once again in the stomach. The stool upon which the man had sat lay tangled around his legs. His body was prevented from slipping away from Charlie's blows by a little runt, no more than fourteen, getting to work on the man's back, alternating the rhythm of his kicks with Charlie's. Nick saw a spittle of blood run slowly out of the corner of his mouth, and began to feel the walls of the room were departing from the floor. He gripped the cold wood of his chair, seeing the glee in the eyes of the young boy as his foot hacked repetitively into Nil's back. He watched as Marten rose swearing, and felt himself slowly rising into the air as if he were one of those Fakirs so respected in this café.

Hassan was quicker than both Nick and Marten, motioning them to sit down with a wave of his long arm. With a few long strides he had covered the distance between them and the tumult. He straddled the prostrate body and, with one arm pushed Charlie to one side, catching him off balance as he had one foot already launched into the air heading towards Nils' uncovered face. Charlie fell into a couple of waiting chairs, while Hassan aimed a stretching kick at the boy's chest, sending him backward into the arms of a helpful stool, and shouted at him to get out. He swiftly turned his attention back to Charlie who was recovering, more from the surprise of the attack than any pain incurred. Hassan caught both his flaying arms in his hands and held them wide apart, leaning his outstretched body against Charlie's until they fell together onto a table looking like a splayed out spider, or the spread of an ink stain on blotting paper. All this time he had been talking to Charlie in a low urgent voice, almost a whisper, repeating Charlie's name as if it were a chant, telling him where he was, reminding him what he was, informing him what would happen if.., instructing him what to do, relating to him what the

Germans were like, cajoling him to keep the peace, his lips at Charlie's ears hissing their words, Charlie twisting his head away as if the words were a stream of small, irresistibly biting, insects from which he had to escape. But perhaps their bites were laced with sedative, because, slowly, Charlie's head began to nod, his sprawled out body began to relax, the air around him began to lose its tension. The two, still entwined, began to rise. Eventually, Hassan let Charlie loose, but left a telling arm wrapped around his shoulders as he guided him out of the café while Charlie rubbed at his wrists as if he had been manacled. He turned quickly to the man who was rising unsteadily, his pale hands brushing at his dusty clothes, the side of his face beginning to blue and swell, and spat a thin stream of saliva between his two front teeth in Nil's direction. It landed harmlessly on the floor.

As the door swang shut behind Charlie, as he gathered up his little runny nosed sidekick, the tension in the café slowly peeled away like the layers of an onion. Both Nick and Marten leant back in their chairs, Nick stretching his arms with an indolent yawn, Marten stretching his face with a nervous smile. The bloodied Nils shot them a malevolent glance as he began to talk to Hassan, hesitantly reaching out to touch his arm in gratitude. Hassan recoiled visibly, feeling pressured by the man's unwanted intimacy, Nils quickly drawing his hand away. In a slightly fawning tone he said, "just wanted to thank you for stepping in there. I would've been finished otherwise. No-one else was going to help..." he nodded in Nick and Marten's direction, Hassan looked over, but only smiled at the two. He raised his voice. "You were the only one with enough guts to step in. Them two're couple of cowards..."

A shadow of anger passed over Marten's face, his lip lifting at one corner, his hand gripping at the arm of his chair as he began to rise, but Hassan had seen him and waved him back, putting himself in the line of sight between the two, saying, "They've got to live here, you don't, and Charlie knows me. He won't touch me, but he'd slice the other two up. He's fucking crazy, everyone knows that here, you shouldn't have messed with him..." during his loud monologue he kept his ear open in case Marten came up behind him, but he was fairly certain that the incident was over. He looked back quickly, but Nick and Marten weren't going to move, they'd heard and seen enough. He turned back to Nils. "Listen, it'd be better if you got out now. He won't do anything for the moment, but he can change his mind..." Nils bit his lip, but noted Hassan's penetrating stare, the tense hardness of his features, and nodded his head in acquiescence. He pulled his cheap anorak onto his shoulders, and, his shoulders slung low, he hurried out of the door and sharply turned the corner, now out of their view. Now it was just the three of them left in the café, Hassan, Nick and Marten. Hassan pulled down a bottle of Ouzo, filled three small glasses - conical saucers of glass balanced on a thin stem, which spread out into an upturned saucer forming the foot - placed them on a small metal tray, and walked over to the two.

He placed two of the glasses in front of the two, smiled at them with an easy shrug of his shoulders, and raised his glass at them. "A quiet evening," he said with a cynical little cough, and all three drained their glasses in one shared swallow. Hassan swept them up onto the tray and returned to the bar where he absentmindedly resumed with his cleaning.

The other two returned resolutely to their drinking. Nick had been cut by the man's remark, partly because he felt it was true, partly because he felt unable to do anything about it, which just went to prove its truth. He looked over to Marten, but knew he would find no solace there. Marten was on one. "The fucking bastard. He comes in here, starts a fight he cannot win, expects us to help him, and then says we are the cowards. And that fucking gipsy, he's not any fucking better. We don't need that kind of shit going on here. When I go out, I want to sit down in quiet having a drink, not worrying about my head getting a beating." Nick sniffed in agreement but he was really too nervous to engage in Marten's outrage. He took another fat gulp of sparkling wine. He almost jumped when he saw Marten staring out of the window, his arm outstretched, his middle finger held stiffly upright, muttering, "fucking arrogant bastards..."

Nick turned slowly in his chair, not wanting to see the inevitable, but there, outside on the street, were Charlie and his greasy little sidekick, sauntering along the pavement. Nick felt cold. They'd seen Marten's gesture. They wandered over to the window. Both Nick

Apricot Juice and Other Stories...

and Marten looked down at their tables, looked at each other, refusing to acknowledge their presence. Charlie hammered on the window. They stared resolutely at each other. Nick thought Marten looked a little pale. Charlie hammered on the window, this time harder. Nick saw Marten's lip curl, his teeth grind, but they still refused to look. The glass sheet almost groaned in its frame as Charlie hit it with his fist. Both Nick and Marten looked up but it hadn't broken. Charlie and the kid were both smiling, the smile of the kid black and broken. He tugged at his jacket and started to pull out a thick bladed knife which didn't stop coming. Charlie pointed at both of them, first Marten, then Nick, and then ran his pointing finger theatrically across his throat. He was a gangster of the worst genre. The kid tried to flash the sun off the knife at them, but didn't succeed. Charlie tugged at the arm of his jacket, jerking him away from the window, almost making him drop the knife, and the two of them began to patrol the street outside the café, marching like sentries one way and then the other.

Marten and Nick watched them uneasily, then Nick suddenly slapped Marten openhandedly across the head. It was a light slap, but it shocked Marten who stared wide eyed at Nick. Nick growled, "You fucking idiot. What we gonna do now?"

Marten sheepishly rubbed at his head, sucked at the inside of his cheeks until he thought they would pop, sighed, and said, loudly, "shit!" He grabbed for the bottle, emptied it into Nick's glass, and signalled to

Hassan, who had been diligently observing them all this time. He came over immediately, the regular blue bottle of sparkling wine hanging by its neck in his hand. The two of them watched as he uncorked it, and placed it between them on the table.

He turned to Marten. Hassan seemed to have an expression of mild amusement playing in his eyes, but maybe he was just scared like them. " You live here. You should know better than that," he stated categorically.

Marten nodded his head slowly, and asked "what can we do?"

"Wait," said Hassan with a shrug. "Wait 'till he's gone or forgotten. He won't come in here, not while I'm here." He turned abruptly away, heading back for the bar. He felt sorry for Nick, he could see he was taking this badly. Too nervous to be hard. He spat on the floor, it had nothing to do with him, nothing would happen here. It would happen outside.

And so they waited, nervous animation producing a stuttering conversation, which kept fluttering away into silence, only to suddenly respark with a new effort, a new comment or jittered joke thrown out in the air. The jumpy minutes peeled away to leave an hour and then a second, with glances shot out to the street and to the square, but the two, Charlie and sidekick, were still there. They were always there. That was their home, their place of business, their place to eat, to deal, to piss. Nick and Marten both knew that they could wait as long as they liked, they would still be there. The dull light of day slowly receded, the air outside growing thick as black blue clouds filled the skyline, their rolling weight threatening to bear down on the land below. As if pushed in by the pressure, the café slowly began to fill with people. Chattering people in groups of two and three, over there a group of women, there a couple, there two keen young men in competition for a single woman, their loud high laughter hanging around them like the smoke from their cigarettes. All oblivious to the predicament facing Nick and Marten. Nick was scared and drunk, scratching at his arm, Marten drunk and angry, occasionally running his hand through his white streaked hair.

Nick, always turning to see who came through the door, suddenly brightened as he recognised a face. He pinched Marten's arm, then shook it, Marten pulled it back grumbling, "what's up now?"

"Look, it's Cihan. Maybe he can help us." Nick was enthusiastic.

"Who is fucking Cihan?" asked Marten irritably.

"The guy who just got in," answered Nick, pointing him out. Cihan looked in their direction, and their eyes met. He smiled and tapped his forehead in recognition. Nick motioned him over and then bent over to whisper to Marten, "he's a dealer, knows Charlie and might be able to calm things down for us."

Cihan exchanged nods and greetings with one or two people in the café, shook hands with Hassan, he used both his hands to clasp Hassan's, and then walked a stubby legged walk over to their table. He was small, but solidly built, wearing an old brown leather bomber jacket over a stained red tee-shirt, with khaki brown chinos, and nondescript blue trainers. His hair was short, black and thinning at the top, but he could have only been in his early twenties. The cocky smile in the rounded face, and the quick, clever eyes, left no-one in doubt that this was not a problem for him. Nick knew he'd been inside, but not what for, and that he was respected in the area. They'd met over a glass of wine which Cihan had spilt over Nick while celebrating his release. They shook hands. Cihan creased his forehead quizzically and asked quietly, "what can I do for you?"

Nick scratched nervously at his forearm, looking at Cihan through the smoky gloom, who'd swung a chair and straddled it, hanging his arms over its back. "It's Charlie. He says he's going to do us." Nick then proceeded to relate the whole story, Cihan, nodding, coughing, tutting and humming to the tale.

After the story was finished Cihan rubbed his thinning pate and yawned impressively. "The man's out of control. He's in trouble with his own people and we've told him too. Look, he's basically retarded, thinks like a kid, gets annoyed, lashes out, then forgets everything in a couple hours. I don't think he'll bother with you two." He put his thickset hand on Nick's shoulder to reassure him, but neither Nick nor Marten looked happy.

Nick shook his head. "I'm not so sure. Can you have a word with him?" He winced at the high pitched whine in his voice.

Apricot Juice and Other Stories...

Cihan barked out a sharp laugh, clicked his tongue in his mouth and winked at Marten. "You got your friend into big trouble, now he owes me one, and you owe him one." He paused, waiting for Marten to look anxious. "It's OK, I'll talk to him. Don't look so worried." He stretched as he rose from the chair, twisting it round with one hand, and slid its seat underneath the table standing next to them. They both watched as his balding pate disappeared into the gloom and out of the door.

Ten long minutes later, he barrelled back into the café, heading straight for Marten and Nick. He chuckled generously as they both looked up at him like two expectant children. He placed his hands on their shoulders and gently squeezed. Marten was the first to ask what Nick hardly dared thinking, "and, what did he say?"

Cihan's innate sense for drama was affronted by Marten's impatience, and his face darkened as a surge of quick anger rolled over him. Nick tensed, and Cihan, seeing the raw fear in the boy's expression, was just as suddenly released from his anger. He grunted, clapping Nick on the back, and proclaimed, "he didn't say anything. I told you he'd forget, he doesn't know you, didn't know anything about you. There's no problem."

Nick looked gratefully up at him and nodded his head. "I owe you one," he said, the uncertainty adding a tremor to his voice.

Cihan looked at the two and held up both hands, "forget it, I didn't do anything. See you around." He turned abruptly on his heel, leaving them staring at his receding back.

Marten tutted loudly, gaining Nick's attention. He gestured arrogantly in Cihan's direction. "Well, we didn't need him, did we?" he said, his tone cruel.

Nick sighed tiredly, he wanted to lie down. "He's alright, and it's better to be sure than dead," he pronounced a little too dramatically.

Marten turned to face him, a caustic countenance etched into his features. "You don't really think they'd have done anything?" he sneered at Nick. He emptied his glass quickly, and began gathering his jacket to him. "C'mon, let's get out of here. We've drunk enough," he said in a more conciliatory tone. Without waiting for Nick, who still had half a glass to go, he marched toward the bar to pay Hasan. Nick decided to leave the glass, pulled on his jacket, and then changed his mind, snatching at the glass and drinking its contents as he ambled over to the bar where Marten was now waiting for him.

Both of them approached Hassan shoulder to shoulder, but he waved them away with a swing of his hand. "It's on the house, you've had enough trouble here." Marten headed for the door while Nick thanked Hasan. He hurried after Marten, following him out of the door.

He was directly behind Marten as Marten turned the corner and walked straight into Charlie with a thump. Charlie took two surprised steps backward, his eyes travelling up Marten's body to his face. They narrowed with recognition, his mouth twisted with a sudden rage. Marten, confused, took a step towards him. Charlie had already began to launch his foot into the air, his leg scissored straight and swinging, until the ball of his foot connected with the side of Marten's head with a sharp slap, sending Marten reeling backward and sideways, staggering past Nick, his temple exploding with a blinding pain, his ankles wobbling as if he were a woman wearing stilettos, until he fell stiff bodied backward, the back of his head bouncing off a car bumper with a metallic clang, his body slumping to the ground, lying there, splayed out on his back, his eyes as wide open as his mouth, and as still as the concrete upon which he lay.

Nick looked down in horror, knelt down in horror, slapped Marten's face once, then again, grabbed at his wrist, trying to feel a pulse, his cheek over Marten's wide open mouth, trying to feel a breath. Nothing. There was nothing. He felt, rather than saw, Charlie moving towards him to inspect his handiwork, his black baggy pants running seamlessly into his tasselled black loafers. Nick's gaze rolled up his body, up his white tee-shirt, stained by a flower of blood, framed by the loose fitting, charcoal black, cotton suit jacket, up over his shoulders to his laughing face. Nick felt the bile rise bitter in his mouth, stood up and turned to face Charlie. Charlie looked at him, eyes narrowed, a mocking smirk plastered across his face. He pointed at Nick, turned his hand over and beckoned provocatively to him. Nick froze. As hot anger rose from his stomach up into his chest, the strength emptied out of his limbs, leaving him furious and hollow, his eyes beginning to water as if he were a small child. His anger suddenly turned inward. A roaring hatred rushing blackly into his head he yelled out loud, the painful tears pricking at his eyes, his stomach rolling wildly, he lurched back a step, blindly turned, bringing back his head and throwing it forward until it met the door sill of the adjacent car with a sharp crack. Darkness exploded in Nick's vision, stabbed through with twisting pins of blue white light. He noticed the sticky wetness sliding down his eyes and knew it was blood, as the ground surged upward, concrete biting into the back of his head, forcing his eyes wide open. He was still, unmoving, the pain and the world gushing over him uncontrolled, he saw Cihan spinning into view, and then Marten stroking his face, garbled words falling from his mouth, then the world and the pain faded away.

Three weeks later found Nick and Marten in their accustomed positions, this time in the "Markstube," hunched over a couple of glasses of golden, frothed topped, beer. Nick's head was loudly bandaged, he had long recovered from his concussion, and apart from the scar that would be left on his head and the cold worm of fear in his stomach, the incident would leave no damage. Even Charlie, when he was about, appeared always to move discreetly and shyly away from both Nick and Marten. Perhaps he had been warned off, or perhaps he had been suitably impressed by Nick's outburst of madness, but he had presented no threat in the last weeks. So the two sat and drank and chatted in easy comfort, letting out the occasional chuckle, or, now and then, raising their voices in mock altercation. Nick looked up and nodded in acknowledgement as Cihan walked in. He ambled straight over to their table, his face as straight as wood, fumbling for something in his pocket. He pulled it out slowly, and placed it on the roughly hewn wood table. It stood there gleaming proudly. It was a bullet. He looked at Nick and said, his voice gravelly with its gravity, "a present from Charlie - he hasn't forgotten anything." The worm in Nick's stomach bit, he blanched and swayed in his seat, his eyes wide with horror. He thought he might throw up. His hand reached weakly for the wickedly shining bullet.

Cihan's arm shot out, his body rocking with laughter, and snatched the bullet away. "Watchout, it's live, and it's mine." Nick looked confused and then the stupid joke flooded into view, Cihan almost doubled up, Marten smiling. He smiled back ruefully, and shook his head, feeling a little red in the face. But the worm was still gnawing at his stomach telling him that, maybe, it was time to move on.

The End.